"Bye, Trey. Tom. Mavis." She gave a brief wave and walked away before the tears came.

While she could still see where to walk without making a fool of herself.

As she ran a fingertip under one eye, she bumped into a man standing at the edge of the grouping of tables. She swung to face him. "Oh, excuse me."

He touched her arms to steady her and jerked back as if she'd burned him. "No problem, although I hadn't expected to run into you. Literally or figuratively."

Sarah's gasp caught in her throat as she looked up into the clear gray eyes of Kevin Nichols. She stepped back and in a low voice ground out, "What are you doing here?"

MILDRED COLVIN is a native Missourian with three children, one son-in-law, and two grandchildren. She and her husband spent most of their married life providing a home for foster children but now enjoy babysitting the grandchildren. Mildred writes inspirational romance novels because in them the truth of God's presence, even in the midst of trouble, can be portrayed. Her desire is to continue writing stories that uplift and encourage.

Books by Mildred Colvin

Redeeming
Sarah's Present

Mildred Colvin

Heartsong Presents

To my readers, especially to those of you who, like Sarah, have experienced the heartbreak and loss of giving a child up for adoption. I admire you for your sacrifice to provide not only life but also a better life for your child. Without two such wonderful young women, I would not be a mother. Also, to those adopted children, like Trey, who have wondered, "Why?" may you understand that adoption is not meant to be a rejection but a loving acceptance—not just once, but twice.

A note from the Author:
I love to hear from my readers! You may correspond with me by writing:

Mildred Colvin
Author Relations
PO Box 721
Uhrichsville, OH 44683

ISBN 978-1-61626-286-0

REDEEMING SARAH'S PRESENT

one

Sarah Maddox clutched the single-page letter to her chest as if it were treasure beyond price.

Ignoring the work waiting on her desk, she again read the scrawl she could scarcely believe had come from her son's hand. How could it be his, when the memory she'd carried for the last eighteen years was of a tiny, red-skinned infant, barely able to keep his eyes open? Even the yearly pictures his mother sent hadn't erased the memory of his birth or the one time she'd been allowed to hold her baby. To count his fingers and toes and kiss his soft cheek before telling him good-bye.

Dear Miss Maddox,
My mom asked me to write to you. My parents told me about the agreement they made to allow you to meet me on or near my eighteenth birthday. We talked it over and decided the best thing would be for us to come to Chicago where you live. We could meet in a public place such as a shopping mall. There's one just off old Route 66 near Ogden. I'm not good with directions, but we've shopped there before and know the area. I printed a map off Google for you.
Since my birthday is March 17, and that's on Thursday, we thought it might be best to meet on Saturday, March 19, right after lunch at about one o'clock. If that won't work for you, please let my mom know. I look forward to meeting you.
Sincerely, Trey Miller

She grabbed a tissue and blotted the tears blurring her eyes. For eighteen years she'd looked forward to this day. For the last several months she'd counted the time until she could meet her son. Now the wait was almost over. Today was March 17. Trey would celebrate his birthday with his parents today. Saturday would be her turn. Just two more days.

The intercom on her desk buzzed before Tricia's voice spoke. "Sarah, I have a call for you from Dr. Jenson."

"Oh wonderful." Sarah jumped up from her desk. "Can you hold on just a minute?"

"Sure."

Sarah stuck Trey's letter in her lap drawer and slammed it shut. She hurried to the door, grabbing her purse as she went. In the outer office, she paused beside Tricia's desk, mouthing the words. "Tell him I'm out."

Tricia's chuckle followed her across the room. As she closed the outer door, she heard her assistant speak into the phone. "I'm sorry, Dr. Jenson. Miss Maddox is not in her office."

Sarah clutched her purse as she stood in the hall trying to decide where she could hide. When Dr. Harold Jenson asked her to the hospital staff's Christmas banquet last year, she hadn't known he was divorced, and she was flattered. He was good-looking, with a successful practice, and drove a flashy sports car. Nurses often gave Sarah envious looks when Harold sought out her company in the hospital cafeteria or at hospital-related functions. Sarah liked Harold and enjoyed the attention, but lately he'd been pushing for a commitment she didn't feel like making. She wasn't sure she wanted to be involved in his problems with his ex-wife and their young daughter.

At the moment, she wanted to bask alone in the knowledge she would soon meet her son. She decided a few minutes in the cafeteria with a cup of coffee to start the day would be a good excuse for leaving her office and hurried down the hall to the elevators.

Sarah went through the line in the cafeteria, glancing over the dining room. She took her coffee to a small empty table. Two seconds later, her heart sank, as over the rim of her cup she watched Harold stride toward her, an indulgent smile on his face.

"I thought I'd catch you here." He pulled out the chair facing her and sat as if she'd invited him. "I called your office. When your secretary said you were out, I figured you hadn't had your morning caffeine yet."

Sarah smiled. "You figured right. So why aren't you treating the little ones today?"

"All in good time. Even pediatricians get a few minutes to chase beautiful women."

Sarah shook her head. "I don't see you chasing women." She inclined her head toward a couple of nurses who walked past, giving Harold a quick appraisal. "There go two right now, and I didn't notice you looking."

Harold chuckled, his gaze meeting hers. "I saw a couple of nurses, but I'm looking at the only beautiful woman in the hospital."

Sarah felt the color rise to her cheeks while she stared at her coffee. "I wish you wouldn't say things like that."

"Why not?" He reached across the table and took her hand. "I've told you how I feel, Sarah. I'd like for us to be more than friends. A lot more."

"I know." She slipped her hand from his and nestled it in her lap. "But right now isn't a good time for me. I've got a lot on my mind. I'm still fairly new at my job, and it's very demanding."

"Personnel director." Harold's blue eyes smiled at her. "Sure, that's a big responsibility, and I'm proud of you. I have no doubt you will do great. You already are. But there's more, isn't there?"

"There's also my son." Sarah watched his expression cloud.

He didn't approve of her upcoming meeting with Trey.

"That's Saturday, isn't it?"

"Yes, in the afternoon."

"What about his father?"

Sarah frowned. "His parents will be with him, both of them."

"I mean his birth father. Will he be there?"

Air rushed into her lungs at the thought. "No, of course not. Why would he?"

Harold's voice softened. "He has as much right as you do, Sarah. Why wouldn't he be there?"

The thought of Kevin Nichols showing up after eighteen years, shoving his way into her son's life after what he'd done, filled Sarah with dread and a touch of anger.

"He won't be there. He didn't care when Trey was born, so why would he care now? I'm the one who was left with the decisions and had the baby. I'm the one who chose the adoptive parents and made arrangements to keep in touch with my son while Kevin finished out his senior year playing football and dating cheerleaders."

Harold sighed and leaned back, keeping his intense gaze locked with hers. "People change, Sarah. That's something you might want to consider. How old was this boy when you got pregnant?"

Heat filled Sarah's face at Harold's bluntness. She thought back to the teenage boy Kevin had been. To the love she thought they'd shared. The plans they'd made. Until they went too far and she'd been caught.

"He was barely seventeen when I told him about the baby."

"Just a child." Harold shook his head.

Sarah nodded, remembering. "We both were. He offered to pay for an abortion. When I refused, he walked away." She looked up at Harold. "He offered to kill his own son. I hated him for years. I was scared; he was terrified. I haven't seen him since before Trey was born."

"That's probably for the best." Harold smiled at Sarah. "I'm sorry, sweetheart. I didn't mean to dredge up old memories. How about I make it up to you? I don't have Katie this weekend, so let's go out Saturday night after you meet your son. You can tell me about it then."

"I don't know, Harold." Sarah forced a smile. "I may not be good company. If you want to call or come by the house, that would be fine."

"Hey, I'll take what crumbs I can get." Harold looked at his watch and stood. "My break is over. Keep smiling, and I'll see you Saturday if not before."

Sarah watched him walk away. She took a sip of her now-tepid coffee and frowned. She needed to get back to work, too. Saturday would be here before she knew it, and that would be soon enough to go down memory lane.

❧

Sarah had no trouble finding the shopping center Saturday afternoon. In fact, she arrived fifteen minutes early. Her hands trembled as she reached for her purse. She pulled Trey's invitation out and read it through one more time before tucking it back and finding her hairbrush.

The car mirror reflected her long, straight hair as she pulled the brush through. According to his pictures, Trey's hair had been blond like hers when he was little, but had gradually darkened, until now it was as dark as Kevin's. With a sharp intake of air, Sarah pushed Kevin's image from her mind and replaced her hairbrush. She unsnapped her seat belt and opened the door. Today was her time to spend with Trey. Kevin had no place in either of their lives. Not even in her memories.

She walked quickly across the parking lot and paused just inside the mall entrance to smooth her hands down the sides of her new black slacks. She pressed one hand against her fluttering stomach and looked around. Shoppers filled the large open area, as they hurried from place to place, ignoring her while she gathered enough courage to take another step. When several people brushed past to go out the door, she stepped out of the way and kept walking, although she was tempted to turn and follow them outside.

She'd looked forward to this moment for eighteen years and now that it was upon her, she would grab any excuse to hide from the one person she longed more than any other to see. Trey's map said they would be waiting in the food court. Would she recognize the young man she still thought of as a tiny baby? If only he wouldn't be disappointed in her. Or be ashamed of her.

Each year, beginning with his first birthday, as part of the agreement she'd made with his adoptive parents, she received a picture of her son and a letter telling of his accomplishments. She always kept the latest picture on her mirror, where she studied his little boy face until she would've recognized him anywhere. When another birthday rolled around and a new picture came, the old one found a special place next to the accompanying letter in her scrapbook dedicated to Trey. But even knowing Trey was now a young man didn't erase the image in her mind of the infant she'd held such a short time before relinquishing him to the Millers.

Sarah stopped at the edge of the food court and saw him immediately. She focused her attention on the dark-haired young man walking toward her. Shock coursed through her at the remarkable resemblance to Kevin. A resemblance his pictures hadn't captured. Or one she'd refused to believe. For a moment she didn't see Trey Miller her son, but she saw the boy she'd given her heart to years before. The boy who'd taken all she had to give before trampling her love into the ground with his rejection of her and their unborn child.

Trey's hesitant smile brought Sarah's mind to the present, and she focused on his face while she forced a smile to her lips. "Trey?"

His smile widened. "That's right, and you're Sarah Maddox, aren't you?"

Her name spoken with an impersonal tone, as if he were speaking to a stranger, caused a heavy weight to settle near her heart. But what did she expect from a boy who probably saw her as an interruption in his life? A boy to whom she was a stranger. She should've never insisted on meeting him. Why hadn't she left well enough alone? She glanced to the side as the urge to flee pulled at her.

"Miss Maddox?" Trey's smile faltered. "Is anything wrong?"

"No, nothing." Sarah shoved her misgivings aside and again smiled up at her son. My, but she did have to look up at him. Never again would she picture him as the tiny baby who'd stared into her eyes so trustingly when she kissed him good-bye. "There's just a lot to take in. Meeting you again, I mean."

He gave a quick laugh and motioned to the side. "Yeah, I know. My folks are waiting over there."

Sarah followed Trey as they wound past several tables before stopping by a middle-aged couple who sat looking as uncomfortable as she felt. The man stood with a welcoming smile and extended his hand. As Sarah shook hands with Tom and Mavis Miller, she recognized the people she'd met briefly when they'd come for Trey. They'd been in their early thirties then, about the same age she was now. Funny how old that seemed eighteen years ago.

"We won't stay." Tom stepped back from the table and Mavis stood. "We figured you'd like to visit with Trey alone."

"Thank you." The anxiety she'd carried all morning eased.

As soon as his parents left, Trey motioned toward the table. "Would you like to sit here, Miss Maddox?"

"Certainly. But please call me Sarah."

Trey nodded with a quick flash of dimples that again brought Kevin to her mind. "Okay, Sarah it is."

She shook off the intrusive image of Kevin and eased the package she carried to the table as she sat across from Trey with her purse in her lap. "I brought you a gift. I hope that's all right."

Trey grinned as he took a gaily wrapped box from a bag at his feet. He handed the package to Sarah. "Looks like we both had the same idea. This is my gift to you. Please, I'd like for you to open it first."

Sarah tore the paper wrapping while Trey watched. She lifted the lid from the box inside to reveal a white leather Bible with her name imprinted in the lower corner in gold leaf. "Oh, Trey, this is so nice. I haven't had a new Bible since I was about fourteen years old. I will treasure this one always."

His clear gray eyes so like Kevin's met her gaze across the table. "I'd really like for you to read it. Mom helped me pick it out especially for you. It has extra helps and study guides just for women. I hope you like it and find a blessing from its words."

"I will. I promise." Sarah didn't specify what she was promising and hoped Trey wouldn't push the point. He seemed like such a nice boy, and she liked that he was interested in the Bible. She always carried a Bible to church and followed the scripture reading there, but she hadn't spent time studying God's Word since her early teen years.

"Good." Trey tore the last of the paper from his gift. He held the picture album in one hand and opened the cover. "What is this?"

Fear he wouldn't understand or appreciate her gift clutched Sarah's heart. "It's sort of a history of your biological family. I hope you don't mind." She shrugged, trying to keep the concern from her voice. "I thought you might like to see what some of your ancestors looked like."

"Wow!" Trey glanced up with shining eyes. "This is way sweet! Are you saying these people are my own blood relations?"

Sarah nodded. "Yes, they are, but I'm not sure how sweet most of them are."

They laughed together, and Sarah's muscles relaxed. She pointed to the first couple. "This is my mom and dad. Their names are David and Linda Maddox. They still live in Litchfield, the small town I grew up in, and they would've been here with me today if they could have. They'd love to meet you. Here's my brother John and his family. My grandparents are on the next page."

When they reached Sarah's high school graduation picture, Trey looked across the table with a question deep in his eyes.

"What?" Sarah held her breath, not sure what he would ask.

Trey looked away for a moment and then back with a half laugh. "So you did graduate from high school?"

"Yes, I did." Pain she thought forgotten touched her heart. "I missed a couple of months my senior year, but was able to keep up and return the following year."

He nodded and stared at the picture. "I see."

"No, I think there's more. What is it?"

He looked up to meet her gaze. "Why?"

For a reason she didn't understand, tears burned her eyes. "I don't know what you want, Trey. What are you asking?"

He continued to stare into her eyes as if trying to see her very soul. "Why did you give me away?"

Each word slammed against her heart. Give him away? Didn't he know how much she wanted to keep him? How she'd ached for him with every fiber of her being for the past eighteen years? But of course not. How could he?

She could scarcely force the words past the lump in her throat. "You were never mine to keep, Trey. I gave birth to you, yes, but I was only seventeen. I had no job, no diploma, no husband, no future for a baby. Oh, I tried to keep you. I fought my parents and the social workers when they told me adoption was the best choice for both you and me. I fought until the day after you were born. I thought I loved you before you were born, but in the last twenty-four hours you were mine, I knew how wrong I'd been."

She wiped a tear from her cheek. "I held you in my arms and counted your fingers and toes. I dreamed of taking you home and watching you grow. Seeing you smile, teaching you to say 'Mama,' and helping you take your first step. I wanted that so much, only I didn't have a home then. I couldn't take care of myself." Her voice dropped to a whisper. "I couldn't take care of a baby."

She touched his hands, which were clenched in front of him on the table. "I'm a stranger to you, Trey, but you've lived in my heart for every minute of the last eighteen years. I gave you away because I loved you."

Trey turned his hands over and held her hand between them. His eyes shone with a suspicion of tears. "Thank you. I want you to know, I think you did the best thing possible for me. I had a childhood other kids can only dream about. My mom and dad love me, and I love them. They are the best." A wide smile split his face. "Now I know where I came from, and that's really sweet, you know? 'Cause in my book, you're the best, too."

Sarah laughed through a sheen of tears. She couldn't be the best in anyone's book. "Thanks, Trey. Your parents did a good job raising you, and I'm thankful. Are you interested in seeing more of where you came from?"

"Sure am." Trey turned back to the picture album with a light of interest in his eyes that Sarah didn't think was feigned.

As they pored over the album, advancing a few pages and

then back for clarification before going on, the time flew. Trey seemed genuinely interested in each picture and the stories Sarah told about his blood family, as he called them. Before she was ready, his parents returned.

"You two seem to be getting along fine." Mavis Miller rested her hand on the table, as she smiled down at Sarah. Her husband stood behind her with a smile just as warm.

Sarah wondered at the sincerity of their friendliness. She couldn't share such a wonderful boy with anyone else, especially not the woman who'd given him life. Weren't they afraid she might steal his affections? She glanced from the parents to her birth son and saw something deeper behind their smiles. Security? Peace? A connection that made them a family? Something she resented and longed for herself.

She stood, knowing her time with her son had come to a close. "Thank you for letting me meet Trey. I've enjoyed our visit more than you can imagine." She gave Mavis a quick hug and shook Tom's hand. Then she walked around the table to enfold the tall, young man in a heartfelt embrace. She choked back tears when his strong arms held her close for a moment. She smiled up at him and spoke to keep from crying. "Maybe we can keep in touch."

He grinned. "Yeah, I'd like that. In fact, I'd like for you to come to my high school graduation. If you don't mind, I'll send you an invitation."

"Of course I'll be there. Just try to stop me." Sarah blinked away tears and managed a smile for both Trey and his parents. They seemed to hold such easy acceptance of her intrusion into their lives that she couldn't help but like them.

Trey held up the album Sarah had given him. "Thanks for the pictures. I like having that background. Especially the medical information. You never know when that might come in handy. But mostly it sort of gives me a feeling of connection. It's great."

"You're welcome." Sarah clutched her Bible close. She would treasure it always because it came from her son. "Thanks again for my gift. You couldn't have given me anything nicer."

He gave a quick nod. "All I ask is you read it often. It holds the answers to all our questions."

"Yes." Sarah turned away knowing she might cry at any moment. "I've got to go, but please, write to me."

"Are you on Facebook?"

At her nod, he smiled. "I'll find you there. Bye, Sarah."

"Bye, Trey. Tom. Mavis." She gave a brief wave and walked away before the tears came. While she could still see where to walk without making a fool of herself.

As she ran a fingertip under one eye, she bumped into a man standing at the edge of the grouping of tables. She swung to face him. "Oh, excuse me."

He touched her arms to steady her and jerked back as if she'd burned him. "No problem, although I hadn't expected to run into you. Literally or figuratively."

Sarah's gasp caught in her throat as she looked up into the clear gray eyes of Kevin Nichols. She stepped back and in a low voice ground out, "What are you doing here?"

two

Kevin kept his voice as soft as hers. "Same as you. Meeting Trey."

Sarah's glare matched Kevin's frown. She started to tell him exactly what she thought of him. He hadn't wanted Trey eighteen years ago, so why would he now? Then she glanced over her shoulder.

Trey stood beside his parents watching. He couldn't hear them, but the troubled expression on his face brought her to her senses. She would not let Kevin Nichols create a scene that might ruin her fledgling relationship with her son.

She stepped around Kevin, turning back with a false smile Trey could see and spoke with a soft voice he couldn't hear. "I don't know how you found out about him, and I don't know why you want to meet him. But remember this. Trey is a wonderful boy, and you'd better not do anything to hurt him."

Before Kevin could respond, she waved at Trey and walked away.

❧

Kevin stared after Sarah's retreating form. Was there ever a woman as beautiful as Sarah Maddox? She'd been beautiful as a teenager, and she far surpassed that as an adult. He hadn't seen her since he'd left for college. Until today. Obviously she still hated him.

He watched her blend in with other shoppers and disappear into a store. Still his heart hammered. He'd known she'd be here. He just hadn't planned on getting close enough to speak. Or to touch her. His hands still tingled from holding her shoulders.

"She's really pretty, isn't she?"

Kevin turned to find Trey beside him, a hesitant smile on his face. Kevin gave a short laugh. "She's more than pretty."

"Yeah, I guess so. Would you like to meet my parents?"

"Sure." Kevin saw a lot of himself in the boy who led him across the food court. He had his height and his coloring. But except for the dimples, Sarah's smile sat easily on his lips. Seemed strange to analyze a person he'd never met, seeing some of himself and some of Sarah in him. But Trey was not just any person. He was the product of a love Kevin once thought would last for all eternity. A love that might have stood a chance, if he and Sarah had waited.

"Hello, Kevin Nichols?" The older man held out his hand. "I'm Tom Miller, and this is my wife, Mavis. We're glad to see you again."

Kevin shook hands with the man, and then the woman. "Good to see you, too. Sorry I'm a little early."

"That isn't a problem." Tom shrugged. "We were running late, but these things happen. To be honest, we didn't expect you and Sarah to run into each other."

"Quite literally, in fact." Kevin's heart still raced from his encounter with Sarah. "She obviously didn't know I'd be here."

"No," Mavis said. "She never mentioned you in a letter, so we respected that and didn't tell her we also corresponded with you."

"I appreciate your willingness to share your son with Sarah and me through the letters and pictures." He turned toward the teenager. "And, Trey, thanks for agreeing to this meeting. Your parents made a gentlemen's agreement with two teenagers that they have honored better than many men do a signed contract."

Mavis gave Kevin a quick smile. "We're not as selfless as we may look. We've seen other adopted children who had no knowledge of their background. They are often like a ship without an anchor. We all need some tie to tell us where we've come from so we can better move into our adulthood. Otherwise there's a void that hasn't been filled. We were glad to provide that for Trey with both you and Sarah."

"I hadn't thought of that." Kevin studied the woman and man who stood before him and wondered at Sarah's wisdom in choosing them. Before she stopped talking to him, she told him the social worker had thirty applications for her to look at. He should have helped her. But he'd been so scared that he'd wanted the whole, frightening experience to go away. So he turned his back on it. An option he now understood Sarah hadn't had. No wonder she hated him.

As soon as he heard she'd had the baby, he went to the hospital. There he saw his son in the nursery, and he also met the Millers. When they told him they'd be keeping in touch with Sarah, he realized he wanted that, too.

He gave Mavis a quick nod. "Still, you could've told me to get lost that day at the hospital."

He glanced at Trey, and a connection he hadn't expected gave him closure he hadn't missed as well as a new beginning he wanted. "I'm glad you didn't, though."

Tom slipped an arm around his wife's shoulders. "Didn't you say you wanted to do a bit more shopping? Let's leave Kevin and Trey to get acquainted."

The couple strolled off arm-in-arm, leaving Kevin alone with a grown son he didn't know. He glanced at the table and chairs but didn't want to sit. Seeing Sarah again stirred old memories that pushed him to run away, just as he'd done long ago.

Trey seemed to be waiting for him to make the first move. Maybe he was nervous. Kevin couldn't fault him there, as he'd never felt more unsure of how to act. How did one relate to a son he'd never met? But Kevin didn't have a son. Not really.

He'd given up that privilege before he was mature enough to be a father.

"I saw an arcade back that way." Kevin motioned over his shoulder.

Trey nodded as he hoisted a backpack. "That's fine. Maybe walking around would be a good idea."

"Yeah, probably." Kevin stuck his hands in his pockets and fell into step with Trey. He noticed Trey moved with the same easy grace he'd always admired in Sarah.

"So, you're eighteen now. That makes you a senior, right?" Kevin mentally shook his head. Stupid question, but what else was there to talk about?

"That's right." Trey smiled. "I'd like to invite you to my graduation if you're interested in coming. It's still a couple of months away, of course."

"Sure." Connecting the baby he remembered with this tall young man was harder than he'd imagined. "Just let me know when and where."

"That's great." Trey beamed at him. "I'll send you an invitation. We'll probably have it on the football field, because there's more room there than in the gym."

"Sounds good. How many are in your class?"

"We live in a small town." Trey stepped aside to let Kevin go in the arcade ahead of him while a group of kids walked out. "I think we have about a hundred and twenty graduating this year."

"That's a good size." Kevin longed to ask if he invited Sarah, but he couldn't. Did he even want to know? If she came, he wouldn't have to see her. How hard would it be to get lost in a crowd that size? He'd have to think of something special to give Trey for a graduation gift, and he didn't know what Trey liked.

Kevin stopped beside Trey as they watched some kids at the games. "Would you like to play?"

Trey's smile appeared sheepish. "Actually, I don't care much for stuff like this. I mean, I play video games once in a while with my friends, but I'm just not into it like some guys are."

"Really?" They turned and ambled from the store. "What sort of things do you do for fun?"

"I play football at school." Trey's eyes lit up. "I went out for track my freshman year and got hooked on running. I guess I'm more interested in something with a little action."

Kevin shook his head, amazed at what Trey had unknowingly revealed. "Sarah ran in high school. She won second place in district her sophomore year and first place the next year."

By the summer after her junior year, she was pregnant with his baby—with Trey. He didn't mention the obvious. "From her looks now, I'd guess she still runs for exercise."

Trey gave Kevin a searching look but only said, "That must be where I got that. Did you play sports?"

"Yeah, I played football, was a quarterback all through high school, and I played a little in college." They stopped back at the table in the food court. "Hey, would you like a drink of something? My treat. Iced tea sounds good to me, but I think they have pretty much anything here."

"Sure, thanks." Trey followed him to the counter. "Tea sounds good."

They settled in with their drinks on the table and relaxed as they talked, getting acquainted. Then Trey asked, "What do you do for a living?"

"I work for an accounting firm here in the city. I've been with Parker Accountants for about eight years. I also buy and sell real estate on the side."

"Sounds interesting." Trey's light gray eyes seemed a reflection of his own.

Kevin laughed. His heart warmed with knowledge that this boy was the baby he and Sarah could have raised if things had been different. "It can be interesting. I'm either rolling in profits or I'm broke. That's why I'm still an accountant."

Trey laughed with him. "I don't know what I'd like to do. I'm going to college this fall. Maybe I'll figure things out then."

"Are you good with math?"

Trey shrugged. "Not bad."

Pride swelled in Kevin's chest. He'd bet Trey was a whiz at math, just like him. "You could be an accountant. Or a math teacher. You'll find something."

"Yeah." A grin lifted the corners of Trey's mouth and his eyes sparkled. "One thing I know. I'll be playing football."

"Is that right?" Kevin grinned. Just like he'd done. "Where are you going to college?"

"Illinois State University."

"That's great. So you'll be a Redbird then."

Trey laughed. "Looks that way."

Kevin took a swallow of tea. "I played at SIU in Carbondale. The Redbirds were worthy opponents back then. How about baseball? Or is that too tame for you?"

"Sure, I like baseball."

"Have you been to a White Sox game?"

"Actually, no. Dad's been intending to take me, but our schedules never have meshed just right."

"Maybe I can take you and your dad." Kevin shrugged. "Your mom, too, if she'd like to go."

Trey grinned. "Yeah, to be honest, she'd probably enjoy a game more than Dad. I think that's been one of the problems with our scheduling conflicts." He pulled a wrapped package from his backpack. "I hope you don't mind. I brought you a gift."

Kevin hesitated before he took the package. "I didn't bring you anything."

Trey shrugged. "I didn't expect you to. Hey, if you get me into a White Sox game, I won't complain."

They laughed together, and Kevin tore the wrapping from

a dark blue leather-bound Bible. Kevin ran his hand over the cover and across his name in the lower right corner. He looked up, meeting Trey's gaze. "This is really nice, Trey. Thanks."

"You're welcome." Trey seemed suddenly shy. "I know gifts aren't supposed to come with conditions, but I'd really like for you to read it at least a little each day."

A lump formed in Kevin's throat. He didn't know what to say. Would he read from the Bible? He didn't know, and he didn't like making promises he couldn't keep. He searched his brain for a way to agree without committing.

"So, how'd it go?" Tom Miller's unexpected voice behind him brought a welcome interruption.

Kevin stood and turned to greet the older couple. "You have a great son, Mr. Miller."

❧

Sarah glanced out the window where she browsed through blouses she had no interest in and didn't need. She had tried to leave the mall. Twice she got as far as the entrance and turned back both times. She wouldn't interfere with Kevin's visit, but she couldn't make herself leave, either. So when she saw Kevin and Trey step out of the arcade, she'd darted into this department store. Now she was stuck here for fear they might see her if she left. She occasionally drifted near the window and glanced out to see if they were still there.

They were, and they seemed to have hit it off great. Too great. But who wouldn't get along with Trey? Kevin, on the other hand. . . If she had her way, Kevin wouldn't get within ten miles of Trey. How could he sit and smile at her son after telling her to get an abortion?

She made a disgusted sound and picked up a blouse for a better look. But instead of seeing the blouse, she saw Harold's face and heard the words he'd said, *People change, Sarah. He has as much right to see Trey as you do.*

She glanced out the window again and saw Trey's parents

heading toward the table. They stopped and Kevin stood. He would be leaving soon. Surely she could slip out without anyone seeing her.

❧

Out of the corner of his eye, Kevin saw a woman leave the store across the way, and his heartbeat increased. No other woman had ever affected him the way Sarah did. As quickly as possible, without seeming to hurry, he told Trey and his parents good-bye, promised to get in touch with them when he could set up a date to go to the stadium, and left.

Had he lost her? No. Her long blond hair flew out as she pushed through the front doors. He broke into a fast lope to catch up. At the doors, he paused when she crossed the parking lot. Keeping well back, Kevin followed Sarah until she stopped beside a late model forest green sedan and got into the driver's side.

All right! He had her now. He turned and retraced his steps to his own car, parked not far away. But as he slid behind the wheel, he stopped. What was he doing? Why did he want to follow her? Even if he caught her or found out where she lived, what would he do? Seeing her after all this time brought her back to life in his mind. Touching her had broken through a barrier against her he'd built around his heart when they were teenagers. But so what? They had nothing left for each other. Their love had died more than eighteen years ago. He slumped in the seat. Nothing remained to resurrect.

He started his car and drove from the mall, turning to the south, the opposite direction from the way Sarah had taken.

three

"You have a call on line one." Tricia's voice cut through Sarah's concentration. "Darlene at the shelter. No doctors lurking today."

Sarah answered the intercom. "Thanks, Tricia, for that uplifting bit of info. I'll take the call."

She heard Tricia giggle, and her phone rang. She lifted the receiver to her ear. "Darlene, hi. How are things going?"

"Oh, the girls are fine right now." Darlene's voice sounded harsh, which was unusual for the soft-spoken woman. "Of course, they may be homeless by evening."

"Homeless?" Sarah straightened in her chair. "What are you talking about?"

"I'm talking about some heartless developer who's coming in here and tearing our home down." Darlene sniffed. "I'm holding the paper in my hand."

Sarah shook her head, trying to make sense of what her friend said. "That's insane. Why would anyone want that old building in the first place? And how could anyone be heartless enough to throw five pregnant teens out in the streets just so they can tear it down?"

"Six, Sarah." Darlene sounded tired all at once. "We took in another girl over the weekend."

"Oh." Sarah propped her head into her hand with her elbow on her desk. She could never understand the heartlessness of some businessmen. Someone with money wanted their building, or more likely, the land it sat on. Why would he care if six young, scared girls lived there? No doubt, he'd never made a mistake so far reaching and irreversible that he had to

25

grow up overnight. Or had to make decisions that would affect another totally innocent human.

The girls had to have a home. Several had been kicked out of their parents' homes, and others had been placed by parents who didn't want the burden of a pregnant teenager. Some had been referred by the state.

Sarah knew she was being unfair to the unknown man when Kevin's face took shape in her mind. Her anger and resentment were toward Kevin, who had participated in her mistake. Yet, now that she'd met Trey, she felt torn in her anger. She could never call her son a mistake. Trey was everything and more than she'd expected. Without Kevin, he wouldn't exist. If only they'd waited until they were old enough to marry. Then they could've kept their child, and this ache in her heart would've been replaced with joy.

"Sarah, do you know of anything we can do? Is there any legal action we could take?" Darlene's soft voice returned. "Should I call a lawyer? I've got the papers, and I don't think there's a thing we can do other than look for another place."

"I'll come by on my lunch hour." Sarah tore her thoughts from Kevin and Trey. "I'm sure you're right, but I want to see the letter."

Sarah hung up the phone and rubbed her forehead. How could this happen to those girls? Only two were giving their babies up for adoption. The others planned to keep their babies and raise them. With help they might make it. With no shelter for support and a place to stay after the babies were born, they probably wouldn't.

Sarah stopped by Tricia's desk on her way out at noon. "I may take a long lunch, but I'll be back in time for the meeting at two."

"Well, I hope so." Tricia grinned. "I'm no good with budgets and charts and such."

Sarah smiled over her shoulder as she headed toward the

door. "Part of the job, Tricia. I'm starting to get used to it."

In the hall, Sarah couldn't believe her bad luck when she saw the tall man walking toward her. When he smiled and greeted her with more enthusiasm than she deserved, she wished she could feel more than friendship.

"Dr. Jenson, what brings you here?"

He fell into step with her as she continued down the hall. The warmth in his eyes frightened her. "I'm hoping you'll have lunch with me."

"Oh, I'm sorry." Sarah turned the corner to the elevators. She pushed the button and waited for the door to open. "I may not have time to eat. I'm on my way to the shelter."

"The shelter?" Harold Jenson gave her a sharp glance. "As in the girls' home you're so fond of?"

"Yes, Harold." Sarah spoke with an edge to her voice. "The home I've supported for the last ten years. The home I believe supplies a great need for young pregnant girls who might end up begging on the street otherwise. Actually, that's probably the best scenario. I can imagine so much worse that could happen to girls who have no family support when they need it most. Someone has to be there for them, and that's what the shelter does in a small way."

He held up his hands as if in surrender before opening the outside door for her. "Hey, I never said anything against your shelter, did I?"

She walked past him into the brisk breeze outside. "I guess not. Sorry I'm so touchy, but someone's going to tear the building down and toss six girls out on the street. I've got to do something to stop them."

His sharp, quick laugh annoyed her, as did his question. "And how do you propose to do that? Does the shelter own the building?"

"No, they lease it. They've leased it for the last ten years I've been involved. Why would anyone take it away from them now?" Sarah unlocked her car and realized Harold waited on the passenger side.

He grinned over the hood. "Unlock the door for me, Sarah. I'm going with you. We'll stop at a greasy, fast-food joint on the way back. My treat. Does that appeal to you?"

Sarah laughed and unlocked the door. So what if Harold didn't stir her blood the way Kevin used to—and still might? Harold was a nice man, and he could be fun. At least he was comfortable. Unlike Kevin, who'd invaded her mind all weekend no matter how hard she tried to shove him out.

She drove several blocks to an older business section of town and stopped beside a large, two-story frame building. Sarah looked at the building with objective eyes and had to admit a bulldozer rammed into the side would probably topple it without a problem. But that didn't matter. This was home to six girls, and had been home to many girls and their babies over the years.

A private institution, Marilee's Home began twenty years before, primarily supported with a trust fund from a donor whose daughter died alone on a city street after giving birth. The grieving parents, whose daughter had run away rather than tell them she was pregnant, started the home as a way to help other girls. The original donors were no longer living, but their vision continued with people like Darlene and Sarah, as well as those who had been helped, and others who believed in the work.

They never turned away a girl in need, and Sarah hoped they would never have to. If she could just get the name of the man responsible for this threat, maybe she could talk to him. Maybe she could at least get him to wait while they found another place to call home.

"We'd better go in." Harold touched Sarah's back, and she realized she was still staring at the old, dilapidated building that suddenly looked like a white elephant to her.

"Yes." Sarah moved toward the back door and pulled it open with easy familiarity.

Inside the kitchen, the aroma of stew aroused Sarah's appetite. She sniffed the air and smiled at an older woman standing at the stove, stirring the contents of a large aluminum pot.

"Hi, Grace."

"Well, if it isn't Sarah and the doctor." Grace's wide smile welcomed them. "Just in time for lunch, too. Go on into the dining room and pull up a chair. I'll have this in there, lickety-split."

Sarah glanced at Harold's amused expression and said, "This would beat that greasy fast-food you were talking about."

He laughed and swept his hand out toward the door leading into the next room. "By all means, let's not pass up home cooking. You can always talk business as you eat."

"Grace, is there any way I can help?" Sarah turned from Harold to ask.

"Not a thing." Grace turned the stove off and slid the large pot to the side. "The girls already set the table. I'm bringing this in now."

"Let me carry that for you." Harold plucked the pot holders from her hands and positioned one on each handle. "Why don't you lead the way?"

Grace smoothed the apron over her ample middle. "Sarah, you should grab this man before someone steps in ahead of you. He's one of a dying breed. Not many charming gentlemen left in this world."

Harold gave Sarah a pointed look, although he didn't speak. Sarah laughed off the comment and said, "Yes, you're probably right, but for now I'm starving and, as usual, can't wait to taste your cooking."

She took Grace's arm, and together the women held the café doors open for Harold. Several young women stood around the room or sat talking at the long table that filled the center floor space.

"Sarah, hi," several of the girls called out. "Are you eating with us?"

"Looks that way." Sarah included all of them in her smile. She saw Darlene standing to the side with a girl she didn't know. A girl who looked way too young to be expecting a baby. But most of them were too young. She remembered Molly, the twelve-year-old who almost died giving birth last year because her body hadn't developed enough for the demands placed on it. Her baby had died.

Grace helped Harold set the stew on a side table, while Sarah skirted the dining table to meet Darlene and the new girl. But before she could, Grace called out, "Come and get it."

Sarah joined the girls at the table while Harold sat across from her. She would've loved to linger over the savory stew and the friendly conversation, but she wanted to talk to Darlene in private. She emptied her bowl and declined a refill when Grace offered.

Darlene stood, pushing her chair back. "Sarah, if you've eaten your fill, I'd like for you to look at some paperwork in my office."

This was the signal Sarah had been waiting for. "Yes, I'm afraid I have. If you gave out doggy bags, Grace, I'd take a bowl home for supper tonight. As always, the stew was delicious."

"Very," Harold agreed. He stood and moved to the side table, where he ladled out another bowl for himself. "You go look at your paperwork." He sat back down and snagged another light roll from the basket on the table. "I don't get to eat like this often enough."

Grace appeared pleased with his praise. Sarah smiled as she and Darlene left the room. Harold had won another admirer, even if she was old enough to be his mother.

Darlene left the door open as she entered her office. Sarah followed her inside and waited while she picked up an envelope and pulled the letter out. She opened the folded paper and handed it to Sarah.

"This came in today's mail." She shook her head. "After all these years in this place, I can't believe someone would buy it out from under us."

Sarah read the letter, which appeared to be a standard impersonal notice of eviction giving Marilee's Home ninety days to find a new location. A construction company had purchased the entire block and would be building a mini mall. She started to refold the letter when the signature at the bottom caught her eye, and she looked closer. Sprawled below the closing, in barely decipherable letters, Sarah saw the name that had haunted her for eighteen years. *Kevin Nichols.*

Blood drained from her face as her heart refused to pump.

"Sarah, what's wrong?"

Darlene's worried voice startled her, and she looked up. She'd been staring at Kevin's name as if he'd materialized in the room. She still didn't know why he'd been invited to meet Trey, and she had no idea what business he had tearing down Marilee's Home. Did he know how much it meant to her? He'd already ruined her life once. Why, after all these years of silence, had he shown up to torment her?

"I'm sorry," she told her friend. "It's just the signature. Unfortunately, the letter seems to be official. I don't know if there's anything we can do, just as you said, other than look for another building."

"What about the signature?" Harold spoke from the open doorway. "Why would a signature make you look as if you've seen a ghost?"

Sarah handed the letter to him.

He looked at the bottom of the page and then at her. "So, your nemesis strikes again."

"I don't understand." Darlene frowned. "What're you two talking about?"

"Kevin Nichols." Sarah took the letter from Harold and handed it back to Darlene. "He signed this, so I assume it's his company who has purchased this block of buildings to tear down."

"You didn't know he was in construction?" Harold asked.

She shook her head. "No, I haven't kept track of him."

"Wait a minute." Darlene looked from one to the other. "Are you telling me you know this Kevin Nichols? Sarah, if you know him, maybe you could talk to him. Maybe you could get him to leave our building alone. What do you think? Could you do that for these girls?"

Sarah turned from the pleading in Darlene's eyes to the bland expression on Harold's face. Could she? Could she face Kevin again so soon? In the distance she heard the chatter of girls' voices and remembered how alone and frightened she'd felt when she learned she was pregnant. Fear had grown with the uncertainty in her life and all the changes her body and emotions went through. These girls didn't need to have their home ripped from them along with everything else they faced.

With a heartfelt sigh, she nodded. "Yes, I know Kevin. I'll contact him as soon as possible and see what I can do."

four

"I need a phone number." Sarah paused by Tricia's desk long enough to add, "For Kevin Nichols here in the city. He may be in construction, maybe a contractor, so you might look in business listings, too."

"I'll do my best." Tricia twisted her chair around to reach the table behind her. She lifted the Chicago phone book and plopped it on her desk. "Might as well start in here. Assuming you haven't already tried this?"

Sarah made a face at Tricia's saucy grin. "Of course not. I just found out at lunch that I need it. The guy is trying to throw our girls out on the street. The least I can do is give him an earful. The most is stop him in his tracks."

Tricia laughed as she flipped open the directory. "Go get 'em, tiger. Give me a few minutes, and I'll get that number for you."

Sarah went into her office and closed the door in case she decided to release some tension with a scream. If only she had the nerve. How could Kevin do this to her? Why would he pick on girls who couldn't fight back? Girls who in spite of the wrong they had done, or maybe because of it, needed understanding and help rather than rejection.

She sat down at her desk and tried to concentrate on her work, but her mind continually drifted back to Kevin. To the man she had seen Saturday, when in her mind, she had yet to give up the image of the boy he had been.

"Sarah." Tricia's voice came over the intercom.

"Yes."

"I found some numbers. Shall I bring them in now?"

"Sure." Sarah glanced at the clock. "No, don't bother. I don't have time. I'll pick them up when I get back from upstairs."

"All right. I'll have them for you," Tricia promised.

❧

When Sarah returned to the office late that afternoon, Tricia stood and walked around her cleared desk. "I laid the phone number on your desk. Well actually, I found three Kevin Nichols that might include the one you want. I hope one is right, but no guarantee."

"Okay, thanks." Sarah tried to focus on Tricia rather than the meeting she'd just left. "Are you leaving?"

"Yeah." Tricia grimaced. "Doctor's appointment. Yearly physical."

"Oh, yes." Sarah nodded. "You mentioned that this morning. Seems like a month of Sundays has passed since then."

Tricia smiled. "I know what you mean. How'd your lunch with Dr. Jenson go?"

Sarah laughed. "You've been spying out the window again!"

Tricia waggled her eyebrows. "Natch, it's what I do best around here. I adjusted the blind and saw you drive off together. Does that mean you've stopped running from him?"

A long sigh from Sarah spoke for her. She stopped in the doorway to her office. "Not really. Maybe if I stopped running, he would stop chasing. Do you think it's worth a try?"

"Only if you want to get caught." Tricia headed toward the outside door. "While most men may be in the running for the chase, I don't think your doctor is. He's really a great guy, and he's looking for wife number two, you know. Maybe you should stop running. Marriage isn't that bad."

Without waiting for Sarah's response, she slipped out the door. Sarah stared at the spot where Tricia had stood and let her parting words replay in her mind. Should she take Harold seriously? Did she want to be anyone's second wife?

She gave a sharp laugh. Did she even want to be anyone's first wife? Harold had never asked her to marry him, but he'd dropped enough hints. She was thirty-five. Almost everyone else she knew was married or had been. Most long before her age.

So why didn't she marry Harold? Tricia was right. Even if she tried, she couldn't put her finger on any one thing wrong with Harold. He was kind, considerate, generous, mannerly. Nothing was wrong with Harold. Except that she didn't love him.

As a friend, he was wonderful. As an escort, there was none better. As a husband, he would be comfortable. And comfortable made good shoes, not men.

She picked the note up from her desk and looked at Tricia's neat handwriting. The name *Kevin Nichols* jumped off the page at her. The room seemed to shrink so there was room for only her, the paper in her hand, and her memories.

She heard the football players calling to each other as practice broke up that day so long ago. Kevin ran across the field toward her. He lifted his helmet and tucked it under his arm. She saw his dark sweat-soaked hair and dirt-streaked face with the welcoming dimples just for her and wondered how she had caught the attention of the most popular boy in school. She loved him so much.

Her hand jerked as a splash hit the note and spread, soaking into a damp circle. She sank into her chair, letting the paper fall to the desk while she covered her face with her hands and wiped the moisture away. The wound in her heart that she thought was long healed now gaped with raw edges. Kevin had done this to her. By showing up at her meeting with Trey and by forcing his way into her life at the home, he brought memories to the surface better left forgotten. If only she hadn't seen him, hadn't felt his hand on her arm. If only she didn't have to deal with him now.

She stood, leaning her hip against her desk for support while she got her purse, took her keys out, and stuffed the paper inside. She'd call Kevin from the privacy of her own home. Tricia's note said she only found residential numbers, so it might be late before she could reach him anyway. Right now, she just wanted to go home.

By the time Sarah parked in her garage and entered the kitchen, she felt numb. She walked through the house until she reached the front door. She unlocked it and stepped outside to retrieve her mail. She flipped through the normal junk mail and circulars, glad there was nothing she needed to concentrate on. Tossing the entire bundle in the trash, she turned left into her living room and sank into the cream-colored sofa, kicking her shoes off as she did.

With her bare feet tucked under her, she curled into herself and rested her elbows on her knees with her head held in her hands. Images of Trey and Kevin flashed through her mind faster than she could follow. She thought of Trey as an infant and as she'd seen him each year in his pictures. She saw him in her mind again at the mall, looking so much like Kevin.

Then there was Kevin at seventeen, holding her hand while they walked to class. Kevin on the football field running with the ball or stealing glances at her when she cheered with the other cheerleaders. Kevin holding her close in the front seat of his car, making promises he didn't keep. Once he'd been hers. Now he could be married for all she knew.

She squeezed her eyes tight against the tears that tried to escape. She didn't want to think of Kevin with another woman. She lifted her head and stood with a sound of disgust. What difference would it make to her if he had a wife and a dozen kids? He could do anything he wanted. She didn't care.

She wouldn't cry over the spilt milk of their past, either. With the phone in one hand and the paper with the phone numbers in the other, she took a deep breath and dialed the first on the list. A woman answered.

By sheer force of will, Sarah did not hang up the phone. She stuttered. "M–Mrs. Nichols?"

"Yes?"

An invisible band squeezed her chest. "This is Miss Maddox with Marilee's Home for girls. I need to speak to Kevin Nichols. Is he home?"

"Ma'am?" The woman's voice faltered. "Are you sure you have the correct number? My husband was Kevin Nichols, but he never had anything to do with any girls' home that I knew of."

Sarah lifted her head and stared at a bouquet of artificial daisies in the center of her table without actually seeing them. "Did you say 'was'?"

"Yes, my husband passed away almost two years ago."

"Oh ma'am, I'm truly sorry." She couldn't keep the lilt from her voice as air rushed back into her lungs. "I do have the wrong number. I'm sorry."

The next number rang four times until an answering machine picked up. She recognized the voice immediately. "Hi, Kevin here. If you're selling something, you're wasting your time. If you want me to call you back, leave a message at the beep. If not, hang up and I won't bother."

Her heart pounded. She'd found him and lost her voice at the sound of his. His answering machine beeped and she jumped. "Kevin, this is Sarah."

Her mind went blank. Why had she called Kevin? Oh yes, the home. He wanted to tear down the home.

"I need to talk to you about Marilee's Home—"

"Sarah? What's this about Marilee? In fact, who is Marilee?"

"Marilee's Home. Surely you know the name of the home you're planning to tear down." Annoyance at him strengthened her voice.

He chuckled. "This is Sarah Maddox, isn't it?"

"Of course." How many Sarahs did he know? Sarah tapped her fingernail. "But what about Marilee's Home?"

"I don't know. You tell me." Now he sounded annoyed. "I don't know anyone named Marilee, and I don't make a habit of tearing down people's homes, anyway. Why are you calling me about this Marilee?"

Sarah took a deep breath. So much for getting off on the right foot. She should have had Tricia call him. She squeezed the bridge of her nose.

"Marilee's Home is a home for girls who have no other place to go. At present there are six girls living there, and most of them are pregnant. One has a tiny baby. You signed a letter telling the director you would be tearing their home down to make way for a mini mall. I read the letter today. I saw and recognized your signature."

As soon as the words crossed her lips, she knew she shouldn't have admitted recognizing his signature. Why would she after eighteen years? With Kevin's ego, he would think she'd pined her heart away for him through each of those years. And she hadn't. Certainly not after the first year. By then she was totally over him. More or less.

"I see."

She waited. Five seconds later, she'd waited long enough. "What does that mean? 'I see.' Will you call off the bulldozers now? You can't be so heartless to shove those girls out into the street."

"I don't know, Sarah. I need more information. I've never liked making important decisions over the phone. Why don't we meet somewhere? We need to discuss this. This is not something that can be fixed in five minutes. Have you eaten? We could talk over dinner. My treat."

Sarah's heart pounded so hard she could feel the pulse throughout her body. Just the thought of being close to Kevin again terrified her.

"No."

In the silence on her phone, she spoke in a calmer voice. "I can't do that, Kevin. Just do something about the girls' home. Please don't push these girls out of the only home they have right now. You don't know what it's like to be pregnant and too young to make it on your own."

Before he could argue, she turned the phone off and let it fall to the table. She clasped her hands together to keep them from trembling.

๛

Kevin awoke on Sunday morning with Sarah on his mind, just as she had been for the past week. Seeing her at the mall, held close in the arms of their tall, young son, had stirred something in his heart. He should have known not to show up early. But he'd been eager to meet the son he'd rejected before he understood what he was giving up.

He didn't regret Sarah's decision to give Trey up for adoption, though. How could he? Trey had obviously had a better life with the Millers than he would have had with a couple of teenagers. He and Sarah hadn't been ready to take on the responsibilities of marriage, let alone parenthood. And he knew now abortion had never really been an option.

Kevin stared at the ceiling and saw Sarah at sixteen. She was so beautiful, and she was his. His dad had cursed when he'd told his parents about the baby. They both said an abortion would be for the best.

That had been his first thought, too, but then he'd seen how the idea hurt Sarah, and he'd changed his mind.

"Sarah won't," he'd said.

"Then let her worry about it."

"We could get married. I've got a part-time job. The baby's not due until March. If you'd help us, we'd make it until I graduate in May, and then I can go full time. I love her, and she loves me."

His dad used another choice word. "As if you snot-nosed kids know what love is."

His mother finally spoke her mind. "Kevin, you are not marrying that girl. I'm sorry for what's happened, but it really isn't your problem. If Sarah chooses to have her baby, then she'll have to take responsibility. This is your last year of high school. Make the most of it. You've got a future, college, and then a real job to look forward to. Afterward, you'll find a nice girl to marry, and you'll be glad you listened to us. For now, I want you to stay away from Sarah. She'll just drag you down. Girls like that usually do."

They talked as if Sarah was totally at fault. Kevin tried arguing at first, but they hadn't listened. The worst was when they refused to help, threatening to cut him off completely if he continued seeing Sarah. He knew he couldn't take care of a wife and baby on twenty hours a week at minimum wage, so he backed off and let Sarah think he didn't care. After his offer to pay for an abortion, she wasn't hard to convince. Her love turned to hate, and although he never forgot her, he walked away and never looked back.

Until a week ago when he saw the woman she'd become.

He laced his fingers behind his head and stared at the ceiling in his bedroom. Was she married? If only he could get Sarah to meet with him, he'd find out. Maybe he could apologize for the past. Maybe he could tell her he hadn't known back then that abortion meant taking an actual life.

When he was seventeen, the baby hadn't seemed real. He hadn't thought beyond getting rid of the pregnancy. Sarah's pregnancy became his enemy. Until he saw Trey in the hospital nursery the day he was born, he hadn't understood he and Sarah had a son. He was so thankful Sarah had enough courage and foresight to let their son live. When she sent word asking him to sign the adoption papers, he gladly gave up his parental rights so his son could have a decent life. Now he wanted to see Sarah again, and he was pretty sure he knew where to find her on Sunday morning.

He dressed in navy blue slacks and a pale blue striped button-up shirt then tied a navy tie around his neck and slipped into dress socks and shoes. A quick bagel and glass of milk became his breakfast before he headed out the door.

The door almost clicked shut before Kevin shoved it open again. He crossed the living room to a small lamp table against the opposite wall and snatched up the Bible Trey had given him. With it held securely in his hand he left the apartment.

Kevin had no intention of trying to start things up with Sarah. Still, a couple of days ago, curiosity had made him find her address. Just to see how she was doing. He'd looked at her street on Google maps. She lived in a nice area, although he wasn't sure which house was hers.

This morning he found her street number on a two-story brick house that told him she was doing quite well. Okay, so maybe she was married. Or maybe she had a good job and was deep in debt.

He drove past her house and circled the cul-de-sac then parked a couple of doors down and glanced at his watch. He couldn't stay parked on the street long without becoming suspect for the neighborhood watch enthusiasts, but if his hunch was right, he shouldn't have to wait long.

A couple of minutes later, her garage door opened, and the same green sedan he'd seen at the mall backed out. He noted, with a feeling of satisfaction he didn't expect, that she was alone. He followed her to a church of concrete and brick that looked like it had served the community for more than a hundred years. He pulled over to the curb and waited until she disappeared inside. Then he parked in the lot and entered church for the first time in eighteen years.

Kevin slipped into a back pew, trying to be as inconspicuous as possible. He saw Sarah several seats ahead on the opposite side. Good, he could watch her without her knowledge.

"Welcome to our church." A middle-aged woman with a wide smile stuck her hand in front of him. "I'm Vera Haines."

He gave her hand a firm shake and smiled. "Glad to be here. I'm Kevin Nichols."

"If you're looking for a church home, you've found a good place."

Kevin's stomach tightened at the thought. "No, I'm just visiting."

"Well, Kevin, I sure hope you enjoy our services, which I believe are about to start. Come visit anytime." The woman smiled again and walked away as organ music began.

Kevin kept Sarah in sight throughout the opening until a voice caught his attention. "We have a couple of visitors today we'd like to welcome." A man stood behind the pulpit looking out over the congregation. "We won't ask you to stand, but a quick wave will help our ushers find you, as we have a welcome gift for you. Tina Higgins is here with her mother. Glad to meet you, Tina."

Kevin watched a young lady near the front lift her hand.

"And Kevin Nichols is here visiting our church for the first time, I believe."

So much for sneaking up on Sarah. Kevin gritted his teeth. He shouldn't have told that woman his name. When the pastor called him a second time, he lifted his hand and caught Sarah's glare across the church. He smiled and wiggled his fingers her direction. She swung back toward the front.

He figured he'd better get to her car before she did as soon as church ended, or she'd slip away from him. He accepted the little welcome bag from the usher and settled back to listen to the sermon.

Almost an hour later, after the last "Amen," Kevin turned toward the door leading outside. He shook the pastor's hand and promised to return as soon as he could. Then he headed for the parking lot.

Sarah wasn't at her car yet, so he decided he'd wait in his. He couldn't blame Sarah for hating him, but he wanted a chance to tell her how sorry he was for all the pain he'd caused them both. The parking lot was almost empty when he finally saw her step out the front door and walk toward her car. He met her at the front fender.

She looked up with a jerk. "What are you doing here?"

He didn't expect her hostile greeting to hurt like it did. He'd gotten over Sarah a long time ago. He didn't need the sweaty palms and pounding heartbeat from his teen years that hit him without warning.

"We have unfinished business. Let's go out to eat and talk."

"No one tells me what to do, Kevin. Least of all you."

He took a deep breath and stuck his hands in his pockets. Okay, he could do this. He gave one quick nod. "Fine, that isn't my intention anyway. But let's get something straight right now. We have a past, Sarah. That isn't going away. Sometime we'll need to talk about it, but for now, let's stick to the present. For some reason our paths have crossed again. You want me to do something about your girls' home, and I'm ready to listen. What do you say? It's up to you."

five

Sarah looked into the adult face of the young man whose memory had haunted her over the years and knew she had no choice. No doubt she'd regret her decision by morning, but today she had no defense against the attraction that had always been her downfall. Only now she was older, without the raging hormones of her teen years. Surely she could discuss business with Kevin without buckling to his charms.

Besides, if she refused to talk to him, he'd go ahead with his plans to demolish the girls' home. She couldn't let that happen. By some slim chance, maybe she could talk sense into him. If not, she'd never have a better chance to tell him exactly what she thought of him.

He spoke before she agreed. "Why don't we take your car to your house so it isn't out in the open. I'd like for you to ride with me, if you will."

Kevin flashed dimples at her, and she looked away. "Since you know where I go to church, I assume you know where I live, too."

"I'll follow you to make sure I don't get lost."

He walked to his car without admitting anything. Maybe she should come right out and ask how he knew where to find her.

Sarah drove to her house and into her garage without once giving in to the strong impulse to look in her rearview mirror. When she stepped outside and lowered the garage door, Kevin waited by his car parked at the curb.

He opened the passenger door for her, and she smoothed her skirt and slid in.

Being so near the one man she had vowed to never speak to again tore at Sarah's nerves until she wanted to jump from the car. Yet here she sat, going out to eat with him. What would her mother say if she knew? She almost laughed aloud at the thought. She'd told her parents all about her visit with Trey, but she hadn't mentioned Kevin's unexpected presence. They never approved of Kevin. Mom especially hadn't. She said more than once he was a bad influence on her. Maybe she was right. Maybe she shouldn't have gone with him today.

"So you're involved with this girls' home." Kevin spoke into the silence, both of his hands gripping the steering wheel. "Are you a social worker?"

"No." She looked behind as he pulled onto the street.

His eyebrows lifted when he shot a quick glance at her. "You aren't a housemother, are you?"

She couldn't stop the quick laugh that brought a smile to his lips. "No, I'm not a housemother. I work at a hospital."

"You're a nurse?" If anything, his eyes widened even more. "I have a hard time seeing that. I bet your male patients never get well."

"Why not?"

His intense look traveled through her heart and stopped in her stomach, causing an unsettled feeling that wasn't entirely unpleasant. She averted her eyes and waited for his reply.

"Any conscious male would love having a nurse with your looks."

"Even if he's only seven years old?" Sarah's heart fluttered from Kevin's words. Harold's flattery never affected her this way. She stared through the windshield at the traffic, as Kevin took an on-ramp to the freeway. "I work in a children's hospital."

"Aw, that ain't fair." Kevin whined so well, she almost laughed. "Here I was wondering how I could get admitted into your hospital."

"I'm not a nurse, Kevin."

He frowned. "Well, if you're none of the above, what are you? A housewife? No, you work in a hospital. So what is it?"

While they talked, they traveled several miles east until Kevin took the next exit. Sarah waited to answer his questions until he stopped beside a restaurant called the Summit.

He shut off the engine and spoke first. "Okay, Sarah, let's do some catch-up. Are you married? Ever been married? Divorced? Engaged? Spoken for? Got a serious boyfriend? What?"

Sarah caught her breath from the shock of his questions. Hadn't they been talking about her livelihood? Why would he care about her marital state? He sat across the car, watching her with a serious expression.

She shook her head. "I don't know anything about you, either."

He shrugged. "I'm single. Unattached."

What did that mean? Had he been married? Did he have children? Why should she tell him anything? She owed him nothing.

She let her mouth curve slightly while her hand found the door handle. "Then we're even. I'm also unattached."

She opened the door and stepped out before he spoke. She bent over and saw he hadn't moved. He stared at her. Did the same thoughts clamoring in her mind run through his also?

She smiled sweetly. "Well, aren't we going inside? I don't think they have curb service here."

Twenty minutes later, they'd been served and were well into a delicious meal. Sarah took a sip of water and looked about the busy restaurant. "Are you aware this place sits beside Route 66? There's a sign on the street right out in front. I wonder if they were in business back when the road was in its prime."

Kevin glanced around. "Looks like they might've been. Anyway there's some Route 66 memorabilia on the wall. Are you a history enthusiast?"

"Not really." Sarah smiled. "Do you remember Tessa Stevens from school?"

Kevin looked blank a moment and then nodded. "Yeah, vaguely. Wasn't she the one who looked like she'd crawled up from the underworld? Never wore anything with color except her lipstick? Black clothes and black hair." He gave an exaggerated shudder. "You were friends with her in junior high before she got all crazy."

"Actually, I've never stopped being friends with her. Amanda Davis and I made a vow to never give up on her. We never did. You remember Amanda, don't you?"

"Yeah." He nodded. "She was your best friend. How's she doing?"

"Fine now." Sarah played with her water glass, turning it with her fingers. "She went back to school for her degree. She quit when she married. It shouldn't be long before she finishes now. But I was telling you about Tessa."

He nodded, watching her as if he was really interested. It could be an act, but she didn't care at the moment. If anyone had told her a week ago she would enjoy Kevin's company, she'd have thought they were crazy. Now she believed she could sit here all afternoon, as long as he kept watching and listening like she was the most important thing to him. She felt like a child starved for love and attention, ready to gobble it up from the first person who offered. But that couldn't be true. Not when she ran from Harold's attention. A person could think too much, trying to analyze every emotion. So what if she shared some weird chemistry with Kevin? That didn't mean a thing. She'd already found that out the hard way.

She took a sip of water and thought about Tessa. "She lives in Texas now, but we keep in touch. She came up here before she married. She and her three boys traveled Route 66 on their vacation."

"And you're interested in the Mother Road now." Kevin

grinned at her and then changed the subject before she spoke. "So tell me, what is it you do at the hospital where you work?"

"I'm the personnel director. I usually sit at a desk and shuffle paperwork, plus a few other fun things. But you haven't told me what you do for a living." Sarah tried to shift the attention from her.

"You went to college, then?" Kevin looked across the table with an intense expression, as if her answer mattered somehow.

She nodded.

He visibly swallowed and looked down at their empty plates. "That's great. Are you finished?"

She smiled. "With college? Sure, that only took four years. I finished a long time ago. It really wasn't that hard."

He laughed. "Cute. I meant with your meal."

She couldn't stop the laughter from bubbling to mingle with his. "Oh that! I will be as soon as you tell me about your job."

His smile deepened. "No big mystery. I'm an accountant."

"Really?" Her eyebrows rose. "You aren't a contractor?"

"Nope." Kevin placed his napkin on the table. "But I do buy and sell real estate on the side. Mostly old buildings in bad shape. Some of those I sell to be replaced. Others I sell to be repaired. All of them so I can get a profit."

"Which brings us to the reason we're here. You obviously intend to demolish Marilee's Home for a profit." Sarah leaned back in her chair, ready to do battle.

Kevin glanced around the dining room. "You know, this place is filling up. Why don't we go somewhere quieter to talk? There are a lot of things we can say, but mostly, Sarah, I'd like to know about you. I think we could spend hours talking and still just brush the surface of everything that should be said. Demolishing your home is just one in a long list of topics."

When Kevin stood, Sarah knew she'd have to wait to talk

to him. Maybe he was right. This wasn't the best place to carry on a conversation that could get emotional on her part. Besides, she had an idea. She let him pull her chair out as she rose, and together they left the restaurant.

When they reached the car, he asked, "Where would you like to go now?"

"My home?" The idea of taking Kevin to see the home he would be tearing down came to Sarah as they left the table. She still wasn't sure it was a good idea.

"Your house?" His eyes lit up while his dimples flashed. "Now that would be a private place to talk, wouldn't it?"

She gave a short laugh. "Forget it. You know perfectly well that's not what I meant. You've been calling Marilee's Home my home, so I did, too."

His eyes widened. "You're talking about giving me a tour of your girls' home so I'll change my mind, aren't you?"

"Of course." She smiled across the car at him. Then she shrugged. "I think you should see what you'll be tearing down. I bet you've never been inside, have you?"

He glanced at his watch. "No, but I'm willing to take a look. Will a ten-minute tour satisfy you? I've got something I want to do afterward."

She nodded. "Okay. That's better than I expected, anyway."

&

Kevin couldn't keep his eyes from straying toward Sarah while he drove to the home. He'd been completely aware of her since she backed her car out of her garage that morning. He didn't look forward to this day's end.

At Marilee's Home, Kevin parked near the old dilapidated white frame building and wondered how anyone could become attached to such a place. A patio of sorts in the back with a privacy fence gave the only access to the outdoors for the girls. Wouldn't they prefer a yard to plant flowers and maybe even a vegetable garden? The area might have once been residential, but businesses had sprung up on both sides of the street. This would be a perfect place for a mini mall. He couldn't imagine anyone choosing to live here.

Once they were inside, in the short ten minutes he'd allowed Sarah, he saw a clean, comfortable-looking home just as Sarah had insinuated. The housemother was a little withdrawn when Sarah introduced him as Kevin Nichols, the new owner. Not that he could blame her. He was, after all, the enemy.

"This is Darlene," Sarah said with a warm smile for the woman who appeared to be in her forties.

She didn't offer her hand, so Kevin simply smiled and nodded. "I'm pleased to meet you, ma'am. Sarah informed me of your plight, and I want you to know I'll be glad to help you in any way I can. Turning you out on the street, as Sarah so colorfully put it, is not my intention."

Darlene's eyes lit up. "Then you've reconsidered? You won't be tearing our home down after all?"

"Why don't we show Kevin around before we talk?" Sarah touched the other woman's arm and motioned toward the next room.

Darlene led the way through café doors into a large dining room. Kevin followed Sarah. Two girls sat at the table, apparently studying from textbooks. They called a greeting to Sarah and gave him an appraising look. The scene appeared as a normal home, except both teenagers were several months' pregnant. In the next room, three more girls lounged on a sofa and chairs watching TV. One of them held a tiny baby. Again, when they glanced up and saw him, he felt as if he'd been judged and condemned. All the girls called a greeting to Sarah. They seemed to accept her in their home almost as if she belonged or was a frequent visitor.

Sarah introduced him to the girls. When she came to the one holding the baby, she said, "This is Kayla. She's holding

Emmie, her daughter who is only two months old. Kayla is attending work skills classes as well as parenting classes while she works part-time and finishes her senior year of high school. She has a full load now, but plans to attend junior college this fall."

Kayla gave a shy smile. "I'm no different from the others. We owe a lot to this place, and we all work hard because of that. But mostly to make a decent life for our children."

Kevin nodded but didn't speak. He knew Sarah was trying to convince him to save the building. More than once, he wondered how she felt after giving up their baby. Even he had felt the loss as a heavy ache gradually lessening through the years. But Sarah had nurtured Trey with her body. She'd carried him for nine months. Surely her loss had been so much greater than anything he'd suffered. Now he knew how she dealt with her pain. No wonder this place was so important to her. Giving time, support, and probably money to help other girls keep their babies and learn job skills most likely helped her deal with her loss.

He listened to their statistics of success and saw the evidence in the girls who were there, but his visit didn't change anything. Before the day ended, he'd have to tell Sarah.

❧

When they left the home, Sarah thought Kevin would say something promising to Darlene. Instead he gave her a tight smile and said, "Thanks for the tour. You have a nice home here."

Sarah didn't know what to do. Should she let him think about what he'd seen first before she pushed him? Not wanting to do anything that might jeopardize any progress she might have made, she simply walked with him to his car and let him open the door for her.

When he slid behind the wheel, she said, "I didn't keep you too long, did I?"

His grinned as he started the engine. He looked out the windshield and shook his head. "Nope. We have plenty of time for one more thing before I take you home. Your dad isn't visiting this weekend, is he?"

Why would he ask such a question? She shook her head. "No. Why?"

He chuckled. "Remember how he used to peek out the window when I brought you home, especially if we were later than he thought we should be?"

"Yes, but we never missed a curfew." Sarah thought back to those nights. "That was one thing he could never complain about you."

"What do you mean one thing?" Kevin acted insulted. "If he complained about me, he must have looked long and hard to find anything."

Sarah laughed. "Your ego is still intact." Her voice dropped to a near whisper. "To be honest, in the end, there was only one thing my parents held against you."

"The baby." Kevin grew serious as he pulled into a line of traffic. "I'm sorry, Sarah. They were right. That was my fault. Back then I'd have done anything I could to change what happened." A soft smile lit his face. "After last weekend, I'm not sure I'd change anything except one."

"What?" Sarah felt as if her throat would burst with the emotion that clogged it so much that she could barely squeeze the word out.

He glanced at her and then back at the road. "I'd have waited. We got ahead of things, Sarah. I should've kept my hands to myself."

They rode in silence for several minutes as Kevin drove east through the city traffic. Finally Sarah said, "It wasn't all your fault, Kevin. I agree we should've waited, but since we didn't, we just have to be thankful we've been allowed to meet Trey. He's so much more than I ever expected. We did the right thing by him. Adoption was the best choice for Trey."

The words were out of her mouth before Sarah realized she'd included him in the decision. Although adoption had not been his first choice, she realized he'd seemed relieved when she told him she wanted to give the baby up. He willingly signed away his parental rights.

Sarah's musings kept her from watching where Kevin drove. He'd already turned into Grant Park not far from Lake Michigan at the beginning of Historic Route 66 before she noticed.

He flashed a smile at her. "Since you've developed an interest in the Mother Road, I thought you might like to take a walk with me right here at the beginning of Route 66. Or as near as we can get to the start and not get run over by traffic, that is."

Sarah laughed with him as they got out of the car. She didn't even object when he took her hand and slipped his fingers through hers. She smiled up at him. "I brought Tessa and her boys here. They loved this park."

They stood close together watching the water spray into the air from Buckingham Fountain. Kevin leaned even closer. "Let's come back some evening when the lights are on. I've heard it's really pretty then."

"You've never been here at night?" Sarah looked into his eyes.

He shook his head. "No, and I can't think of anyone I'd rather be with the first time I see it."

Sarah watched the water spray catch a ray of sunshine and tried to sort through the confusing thoughts and feelings the day had brought. Did she hate Kevin or love him? For eighteen years she'd nurtured hatred, but she felt no hatred now. She felt the warmth of his palm against hers and wanted to cry out at the conflicting emotions she didn't understand. She couldn't fall in love with him again. She just couldn't.

six

"Sadie has a secret angel." Groucho the clown, alias Dr. Harold Jenson, frowned over the heads of a dozen small patients at Sarah in her clown costume. They were gathered in the children's activity room.

Sadie the clown clutched her oversized red purse close and scowled at Groucho. "Hush, you tattletale clown. It's my angel I caught, and I ain't gonna share neither."

"Make her share." Groucho told the kids, bringing a cheer and a rush toward Sadie. "Make her show you her angel."

Sadie shook her head but soon gave in to the eager little faces surrounding her. "Oh all right. But only one at a time gets to see my special angel. And you gotta keep my secret. Promise?"

A little girl leaned against her knee. Sarah moved the bright red purse to her lap and opened it. She reached inside slowly to stretch out the suspense, then pulled a hand mirror to the top so only the first child could see. The little girl's eyes grew wide and she covered the "Oh," that escaped her mouth with a chubby hand.

Sadie smiled at the child. "Now don't you tell who my angel is."

One by one the children looked into the mirror to see who Sadie's angel was. Some were surprised, while others scoffed that they already knew, but all walked away with a smile.

While Sadie showed her angel, Groucho attempted to blow up a balloon, letting the air out several times to the children's delight. Finally he got the job done, and he pretended to tie a thick cord to it. He held the balloon by the knotted stem with the cord loosely wrapped around it. As the last child left Sadie's mirror, Groucho began walking around the room among the children, holding his balloon high.

"Don't reckon anyone wants a balloon." His oversized lips painted in a permanent frown emphasized his negative attitude.

He spoke over the children's cries of "I do."

"Nope, reckon not. Might as well pop this one." He fumbled in a deep pocket in his overalls. "Gotta pin here somewhere."

"I'll take it, Groucho!" A boy of about ten years jumped toward the balloon still held high in the clown's hand.

"Oh." Groucho acted as if he'd just seen the boy. "You want a balloon?"

"Yes."

Groucho lowered the balloon until the string dangled in front of the boy. "Here, take this."

When the boy grabbed the string, Groucho walked away with the balloon still in his hand. The boy's expression was priceless as he stared at the limp string he held, then up at Groucho, who carried the balloon out the door into the hall. Sadie ran after him. After a stunned moment, the nurses in attendance, the children, and the boy holding the string began to laugh.

Before their laughter faded, Groucho returned with three helium-filled balloons in each hand. Sadie followed with six more. They passed them out to each of the children before taking their leave amidst applause and requests to return.

"That went well, didn't it?" Harold smiled at Sarah, although his painted frown overshadowed the smile.

"Yes, like it always does. The kids love Groucho and Sadie. Except when they're afraid of them." Last week a little girl cried so hard when she saw them, the nurse had to take her back to her room. This group of kids had been cooperative and a lot of fun to work with.

"That doesn't happen too often." Harold paused at the

intersection of another hall. "I never thought I'd make a good clown, but I'm glad you talked me into it. Laughter is good for the kids. You can't deny that."

"I'm glad you agreed." Sarah gave him a smile. "Here's where we part. I'll see you later, Harold."

Sarah turned to the right while Harold went left. She'd done some clowning in college and loved the freedom it gave to let herself go. When she became Sadie, she was an uneducated clown who got to hold the little ones occasionally and above all give them something to laugh at when life had dealt them a raw deal.

In the ladies' lounge, Sadie became Sarah again and cleaned the makeup from her face. She packed her red nose and oversized plastic glasses as well as her red and green hair, colorful dress, striped stockings, and red shoes in the large bag she carried.

Finally ready to face the business world again, she headed back to her office and the sandwich waiting to be consumed in what was left of her lunch hour.

Tricia glanced up with a smile. "How'd it go?"

"The kids were great. We had a lot of fun." Sarah flashed a smile as she walked past. "Groucho didn't even ask Sadie for a date."

Tricia laughed. "Cute, Sarah, but not so fast. Who's Kevin? He wouldn't be the phone number I looked up for you last week, would he?"

Sarah stopped cold, her hand against her chest. "Kevin? Why do you ask?"

"Because he called while you were gone. He said you already have his phone number, but I wrote out the message just as he gave it to me. He sounds awfully sure of himself. But then maybe he would be since he says he wants to discuss the home." She shrugged. "You'll have to be the judge. It's on your desk."

"Okay. Thanks, Tricia." Sarah crossed the threshold into her office while her heart picked up its beat. What could Kevin want now? For three days she'd pushed him from her mind, only to have him intrude again. She saw the paper on her desk and picked it up as she sank into her chair, her lunch forgotten.

> *Be ready Friday night at seven. I'll pick you up at your house. We need to talk about your home. Oh, wear something nice, and I'll treat you to dinner.*

Sarah sat and stared at the note. What should she do? Was there anything left to talk about? Kevin said the contracts had been signed. He'd already said there was nothing he could do.

She didn't know Kevin's phone number. A quick search of her purse turned up everything except the paper Tricia had given her with his number on it. She'd have to wait until she got home to call him and cancel. And cancel she would, because she refused to spend any more time in Kevin's presence than she had to.

That evening at home when Sarah called Kevin, his phone rang with neither him nor the answering machine picking up. After trying three times, she muttered, "Why won't he answer? I know he has an answering machine."

When she went to bed a few minutes later, she saw the Bible Trey had given her on the bedside table and picked it up. She ran her hands lovingly over the smooth leather, thinking of the young man who had her smile and Kevin's dimples. What a joy he must be to his parents. What a joy he could have been to her. A mist covered her vision, and she blinked it away. She mustn't think that way. Giving Trey up was the best thing she'd ever done.

She opened the book to the Psalms and read the twenty-third chapter. " '*The Lord is my shepherd; I shall not want. He maketh me to lie down in green pastures. . . .*' "

Did God truly watch over His children and supply their needs like the verses said? She'd drifted from His presence over the years, but maybe she needed to do more than attend church on Sunday morning. By the time she finished reading and praying, her eyes were drooping, and she went to sleep with a strange feeling of security she hadn't experienced for several years.

ૐ

When Sarah still hadn't reached Kevin by Thursday evening, she gave up. Unless he'd changed, he'd be on her doorstep at seven the following evening, expecting her to be ready. That evening, she searched her closet for something suitable to wear and finally settled on a navy blue dress with matching two-inch heels.

Friday evening when her doorbell rang, Sarah's heart lurched, and although she'd been listening for the sound, she startled and hurried to the door. In the entrance hall, she stopped and steadied herself with her hand against the wall. Kevin meant nothing to her. They were only having a business dinner.

Taking a couple of deep breaths, Sarah forced herself to relax. She could do this. She could go out with Kevin and keep her mind on the home. Truly she could. With a trembling hand, she opened the door.

"Hi." He smiled, and her heart thudded.

"Hi." Her lashes shuttered the emotion that must be shining in her eyes. Oh how mature! Her mind flashed back twenty years to her first date. Kevin took her out to eat that night, too. At the local drive-in. He'd just gotten his driver's license, and she'd felt so grown-up to be car dating. Something was wrong here. She didn't want to feel like a fifteen-year-old girl all over again.

Her chin lifted and her eyes opened wide, meeting Kevin's searching gray eyes. "Well." She spoke over the pounding in her chest. "I'm ready if you are."

She clutched her purse in her hand and stepped out, pulling the door closed. "So where are you taking me tonight to discuss our business?"

He smiled and tucked her hand under his arm as they walked to the curb where his car waited. "I assume you've moved past carhop service, so I thought of Latarini's. I think you'll like it."

She could have moved her hand, but didn't. Maybe his mention of their past shocked her into leaving it there. Maybe her memories, and obviously his, kept her from rebelling. Maybe she just liked the feel of his suit coat under her fingers. She allowed him to lead her to the passenger side and help her in. Kevin had always been a gentleman. His thoughtfulness chipped away at her resentment.

At the elegant Italian restaurant, she was surprised to discover Kevin had reservations. The maitre d' led them to a table on one side and waited while Kevin held Sarah's chair then seated himself. The round table, covered by a white linen cloth, held a tall crystal vase with one long-stem yellow rose. Sarah felt as if she was being courted.

"Kevin." She looked over her menu at him. "Why are you doing this? We could have discussed the home over the phone. Why did you bring me here? This will cost you a fortune."

He chuckled. "Right now, Sarah, I have a fortune, more or less. Relax and enjoy the evening. Tell me, when was the last time you dined in a place this grand?"

Sarah looked across the room at the luxurious furnishings from the elaborate chandelier in the center of the dining room to the plush carpeting under their feet. She thought of Harold and shoved guilt aside. She could eat like this more often if she'd give the doctor even a hint of encouragement. She didn't want to, though, partly because she felt uncomfortable with the idea of becoming a stepmother, but mostly because with the wrong person, rich surroundings turned to dust.

When she met Kevin's gaze without answering, he lifted his eyebrows and shook his head. "I thought as much. Why don't you look at the menu and stop worrying about my motives. I assure you, they are pure as the driven snow."

"Sure, snow in April," Sarah muttered under her breath and heard Kevin's chuckle.

"None of that, Sarah." He shook a finger at her. "Remember that snow we had the last of April when we were kids? We even built a snowman."

"Yes, and it lasted until the next day when the sun came out." They'd had fun. She and Kevin. Amanda and Chad. That was the year before Trey was born. The two couples had done so many fun things together. They'd made a lot of plans. Plans that never materialized for any of them. She'd thought Amanda and Chad would make it, but they broke up after they went to college.

She lowered her menu and asked, "You and Chad were good friends. As close as Amanda and me. I've totally lost track of Chad. Do you know what happened to him?"

Kevin shrugged. "Not really. I heard he became a teacher."

"Did he ever marry?"

Kevin nodded. "That I do know, because I was his best man."

"Have you ever been married?" She knew she shouldn't care, but she had to know.

He grinned. "Nope."

She couldn't stop the smile that lifted the corners of her mouth any more than she could stop her next question. "Why not?"

The gray of his eyes seemed almost blue as they swept over her features. His smile disappeared. "Let's just say I've never found another woman as beautiful and as appealing as you, Sarah."

A discreet clearing of the throat brought their attention to a waiter who stood at Kevin's side. "Would you care to order, sir?"

Sarah chose salmon, while Kevin ordered steak. For a while their conversation turned to less personal things, such as the restaurant, their food, and the live band playing across the room. Once Sarah mentioned Marilee's Home, but Kevin brushed her concerns aside.

"Let's talk about that later. Maybe after the theater."

Sarah smiled. "You're taking me to see a movie?"

"Certainly, if you like." Kevin winked at her. "I'm guessing you still like to watch the big screen. When was the last time you went to the theater, Sarah?"

"Are you trying to check out my dating schedule?" Sarah laughed.

Kevin's eyebrows shot up. "Oh, so you have a schedule. Not that I'm surprised. You must have admirers standing in line begging for your attention."

"Hardly." Sarah couldn't stop another giggle from bubbling out at the thought. She hadn't had so much fun in ages. "But for your information, I do occasionally go out. And no, there's no one special in my life. That's one thing I don't intend to change."

Most of Kevin's comments were more teasing than serious. Sarah took them for what they were and didn't worry about any underlying meaning as he joked with her about the fictitious men in her life.

Kevin wasn't such a bad sort after all. She'd been angry with him for too many years. But his charm broke through her defenses. Maybe Harold's comment that they'd been children when Trey was born caused her to see him in a different light. She remembered how frightened he'd been when she told him about the baby. No wonder he suggested abortion. At least he never mentioned it again.

On the way to the theater, their conversation moved to Trey, and Sarah recognized pride in Kevin's voice. "He's a great kid,

Sarah. His parents have to be so proud of him. They've done a good job."

"Yes, they have." An unexpected pang of loss struck her so she looked out the window. "I try to imagine what it would've been like if I'd been able to raise him, but I can't."

"I know."

She looked back at him and saw a muscle twitch in Kevin's jaw. She waited, but he didn't say anything more, and she wondered what he was thinking. They arrived at the theater, and the moment was gone.

When they walked down the darkened aisle, Kevin's hand at the small of her back felt warm and more natural than she'd expected. They took their seats, and she leaned close to say, "Remind me that we are here to talk about the home."

He gave her a blank look for a moment and then smiled. "Yes, that's a good idea, but maybe we should wait until later. Okay?"

So he hadn't planned to discuss the home after all. Why, then, had he invited her out? She should be angry, but she wasn't. She nodded and smiled because she couldn't help reacting to those dimples that hadn't lost their appeal. She was so glad Trey had inherited Kevin's dimples. Just wait until he got to college. He'd have more girls chasing him than he could handle. She giggled at the thought.

"What's funny?" Kevin leaned close and took her hand in his. "I know it can't be the movie."

Sarah focused on the screen and shook her head. She'd laughed during a rather dry confrontation between two men plotting a prison break. "Oops, now you know I wasn't listening. Actually, I was thinking about Trey. Did he tell you if he has a girl?"

Kevin's grin widened, and he squeezed her hand. He whispered back, "No, but if he ever does, I'll let you know."

"Okay, you do that." She settled back and watched a movie

she could have lived very well without seeing. Most of the scenes moved across the screen without her attention. How could she concentrate on the perfect crime when Kevin Nichols held her hand? For the next two hours, she became the seventeen-year-old girl who loved Kevin more than anyone or anything, as if the last eighteen years had been deleted from her memory.

The movie ended and the lights came on, both literally and figuratively. As they walked out of the theater, Sarah knew she had fallen for Kevin's charms again, just as she had so long ago. She let him guide her outdoors and help her into his car.

"Would you like to go anyplace else?" He smiled across the seat as if nothing had changed. As if he'd really intended to talk about the girls' home. Had he used it as an excuse— for what? They couldn't renew an old love that had died so long ago. Dead and buried. That pretty well summed up their relationship.

She shook her head. "No, I think we've done enough."

Kevin didn't speak while he drove across the city. He kept his hands on the steering wheel and, Sarah supposed, his mind on the traffic. She leaned her head back and closed her eyes until he turned and slowed his speed. With a smile her way, he found her street, pulled into the driveway, and stopped.

He put his hand on the seat behind her. "You look tired."

She smiled. "I hope you don't consider that a compliment."

He chuckled. "On you, even tired is beautiful."

He opened his door and circled the car without waiting for her to respond. She wouldn't have known what to say anyway. They walked to her front door, and he waited until she had it unlocked.

He leaned forward and kissed her cheek. "Thanks for the best time I've had in a long time."

With a quick smile, Kevin walked to his car while she stood in her open doorway watching him. His taillights were two red dots at the end of the street before she stepped in and secured the door. She leaned her head against the hard wood and closed her eyes. Kevin Nichols had always held the key to her heart. Eighteen years ago, his rejection had locked every romantic notion she'd ever had inside, and that's the way she wanted it to stay. Never again could she subject her heart to the pain that loving Kevin caused.

seven

Sarah didn't expect to hear from Kevin on Saturday, but Sunday morning in church, she kept glancing toward the back in case he showed up. He didn't.

Monday and Tuesday passed without a word from him. Wednesday morning Tricia buzzed over the intercom that Sarah had a call from Dr. Jenson. She hadn't heard from Harold all week, either.

"Thanks, Tricia. I'll take it." Sarah pushed the button and lifted the receiver. "Hello, Harold."

"How's Sarah today?" His voice sounded warm and confident over the phone.

"I'm fine. Just digging into the routine."

He laughed. "I hope your work isn't as boring as you make it sound."

"Not really." What could he want? Did pediatricians have time to chat between patients? No wonder she always had to wait so long at the doctor's office. "At least I have enough to keep me busy."

"Ah yes, then I'll get right to the point."

Chalk one up for Harold. He could take a hint. She smiled to herself and waited without comment.

"How would you like to visit a museum with my daughter and me? Katie has a history project at school. She has to tour a museum and write a story about life around the time of the Chicago fire. I hope you'll say yes. Katie would like to see you again."

Sarah visualized Harold's young daughter and sighed inwardly. She'd met the child once briefly. Katie probably didn't remember, but maybe Harold was right. Maybe she was bored.

"Sure," she said. "When did you have in mind?"

"Tomorrow evening. Her story is due next week. That gives her the weekend to work on it. How does five thirty sound? We'll grab a bite to eat first since the museum stays open until eight."

Sounded very domestic in a stifling sort of way. Sarah cringed. What was wrong with her? Harold had been nothing but nice from their first encounter. His daughter held top priority in his life and she understood. She would have been the same if she'd been able to raise Trey. Little Katie Jenson would never be a substitute for Trey in her heart, though. No child would.

She focused on the answer she knew Harold expected. "That'll work fine. I'll look forward to tomorrow."

"Great. I'll let you get back to work. We'll see you tomorrow. Oh, and Sarah, wear something casual."

Sarah hung up and stared at the phone for a moment. What had she done? A date with Harold's daughter coming along? She might as well have told him she'd think about marriage.

The following evening when Harold picked her up, Sarah turned toward the backseat, where the nine-year-old sat with her arms folded across her chest. "Hi, Katie. How nice to see you again."

Katie glanced toward her father as he slid behind the wheel and twisted her mouth as if considering before she said, "Yeah, it's nice seeing you again, too. Dad, I'm really hungry. Can we go eat now?"

"Sure, we're on our way." Harold started the car as if oblivious to his daughter's underlying words. But Sarah heard her loud and clear. She settled back in her seat, expecting to be ignored by Katie Jenson.

They stopped at a family-style restaurant that couldn't begin to compare with the restaurant Kevin had taken her to Friday evening. The noise level was louder, and there seemed to be constant movement. Sarah soon discovered that watching children and parents interact provided a welcome distraction from Katie's scowl.

Harold obviously had no clue of Katie's resentment toward Sarah intruding on her time with him. His grin included them both. "So what'll it be? Spaghetti, lasagna?"

Katie rolled her eyes. "Pizza, Dad. Their specialty is pizza. Pepperoni and Canadian bacon."

She jerked her head toward Sarah. "You and your girlfriend can have something else if you want."

Harold laughed, but Sarah lifted her eyebrows. The child needed discipline rather than encouragement. Katie leaned back in her chair and met Sarah's gaze. An emotion flashed through her eyes before settling into a smirk, as if she felt she had set Sarah in her place. What was that first emotion? Fear? Anger? Pain?

Maybe all three rolled into one. Her parents had only been divorced a year. Unexpected compassion for the child filled Sarah's heart, as she thought of her own early life. She'd been raised in a loving Christian home. Her parents seldom disagreed, let alone fought. They never hesitated to show their love for each other or for each of their children. They had stood beside her when Trey was born and cried with her when she gave him up. Even now they longed for their chance to meet him.

How could she possibly understand the trauma Katie Jenson had gone through? At the impressionable age of nine, her two homes pulled in opposite directions. She'd seen Katie's mother once at the hospital with Harold and was surprised by the vindictive spirit she displayed. She could well imagine her turning her child against her father and any friends he might have. No wonder Katie resented Sarah's presence. If her dad remarried, she could safely assume her life would again be sent into a whirlwind of turmoil.

Sarah smiled at Katie. "I have to admit pizza sounds appealing, but I haven't had lasagna in ages, so I think that's what I'll have."

Harold sighed. "This is tough. I like lasagna, but I'm going to have to go with Katie on this one. Pizza is my choice, too. Especially bacon. I'm telling you, those Canadian pigs make the best bacon I've ever eaten."

Katie's blue eyes lit up and she giggled. "Oh Daddy, you're being funny. I'm just a kid, and I know pigs are the same no matter where they live."

Sarah smiled. So Harold understood his daughter more than she'd given him credit for. By choosing pizza, he reinforced his commitment to her.

Later, Katie looked at Sarah's plate of lasagna while she chewed and said, "If you want, Sarah, you can take a slice of pizza. It's really good."

"Thank you, Katie." Sarah felt as if she'd smiled enough to be crowned Miss America, and the evening had only begun. "I believe I might try a small one."

The pleased expression on Harold's face told her she'd made the right decision. Maybe an extra jog around the block tomorrow would take care of all the calories she consumed tonight. She bit into the spicy, flavorful wedge and closed her eyes. "Mmm, this is good."

"See, I told you, you should've ordered pizza."

Sarah opened her eyes to another smirk. Only this one was different somehow. The icy glare had turned into a warm blue twinkle. Tempted to believe Harold's daughter had warmed up to her, but knowing nothing in life could be so easy, Sarah laughed. Her heart thrilled when first Katie's and then Harold's laughter joined hers.

"Daddy says you and him are clowns. Are you really?" Katie

made the initiative for the first time, and Sarah almost held her breath when she answered.

"Yes, that's true. I'm Sadie, and this is Groucho." She motioned toward Harold. "Once in a while we perform for the children in the hospital. They seem to like it."

"I bet you're good." Katie wrinkled her nose. "They wouldn't like it if you weren't."

Sarah's surprised gaze met Harold's confident one as the realization hit her. He expected Katie to like her. They ate and talked about some of the skits they performed as Sadie and Groucho, while Sarah's suspicions grew. Harold Jenson was an intelligent man. He knew he couldn't marry a woman Katie didn't like. He also knew Katie would reject any choice he made, until she got to know the woman. Harold wanted to remarry, and he was counting on this outing, along with a few others, to win his daughter over. Sarah wasn't sure she liked being set up.

Unbidden thoughts of Friday evening flashed through Sarah's mind as they left the restaurant and drove to the museum. Her evening with Kevin had thrummed with an energy that kept her aware of him. Intense awareness of her feelings toward him, whether anger or. . .

The word *love* pushed to the front of her mind, but she shoved it back. No, she didn't love Kevin Nichols. She'd already decided any love she'd felt for him was dead and buried, and that's where it would stay. All the intense emotion remembered from Friday night had been leftover hate toward a man who'd wronged her and their son. She had no room left to love Kevin.

She mentally turned her back on thoughts of past love and concentrated on Harold and Katie as they walked through the museum and looked at nineteenth-century Chicago. Maybe the three of them could make a family. Katie had warmed up to her much more than she'd expected. She even grabbed her hand at one point to drag her across the hall to another exhibit.

They saw sepia-toned pictures of wood-framed houses lining rutted dirt streets and people walking or riding in wagons and buggies. Katie chattered nonstop about everything she saw. Then Harold called her over to another display.

"Look, Katie, here's your story about the fire." As they joined him, he pointed at a picture. "This shows what the city looked like just before the fire. Here's another that shows the destruction right after."

When Katie decided she'd seen enough, they drove to Sarah's house in the early darkness of evening. Harold parked in the driveway, and Katie waited in the car while he walked Sarah to her door.

"You have a sweet daughter, Harold." Sarah held her keys in her hand. "I enjoyed being with her." She gave a short laugh. "It's nice to see a healthy child for a change. Thanks for taking me."

"Yeah. Thanks for going with us. It wouldn't have been the same without you." They stopped on the porch. Harold waited until Sarah unlocked and opened the door.

What she'd said was true. She had enjoyed the evening. Katie relaxed with her much sooner than she'd expected, yet her acceptance stirred Sarah's emotions in a way she didn't understand. She should be glad, but at the moment, she wanted to run inside and close Harold and his daughter out. Instead, she pushed her front door open and waited, hoping he wouldn't lead her into an area she wasn't ready to enter.

"Tonight feels like spring, doesn't it?" His words surprised her.

She nodded. "Yes, even the shower we had earlier today is typical for April."

"That's true." He chuckled. "You know something else that's typical of spring?" Before she could answer, he went on. "Baseball. The White Sox have a home game on the sixteenth. That's a week from Saturday. I should have Katie again then. Would you go with us? She loves outings, so I'm sure she'll be on her best behavior." His voice dropped to a husky almost whisper. "I know I will be."

Sarah laughed and knew she shouldn't have. Poor Harold. He was such a nice guy. Why couldn't she react to him the same way she did Kevin? The question formed in her mind without warning. She caught her long, unbound hair and hooked it behind her ear as she held her smile in place.

"Yes, of course. I enjoy our friendship, and don't worry about Katie. I'm sure we'll get along fine, just like we did tonight."

"You did, didn't you?" Harold looked pleased. Then he shrugged. "But I always figured you would."

Sarah leaned forward and whispered as if imparting a secret. "I know you think it's my great personality that got to her, but the truth is, she's just enamored with meeting the real Sadie."

Harold laughed. "You're joking, but with a nine-year-old, you never know."

The nine-year-old took that moment to open the car door and call out, "Daddy, are we going now?"

"I'll be right there." Harold stepped off the porch then turned to whisper, "Well, so much for my night-night kiss."

Sarah giggled. "I'm sure Katie will give you a kiss when you tuck her in for the night."

He shook his head as he walked away. "It isn't the same, Sarah. It just isn't the same."

Sarah stepped inside her house and turned on the lights. She closed the door and silently thanked Katie for calling her daddy away.

&

"Kevin, you kept me waiting." Valerie Parker's lower lip stuck out in a pretty pout as she rose from the chair behind his desk.

He walked through the doorway in the partition separating his work area from the rest of the large room and tossed a stack of files on his desk before he turned to his boss's beautiful daughter.

"Now why would you be waiting for me?"

She walked behind him, trailing a finger across his shoulders. "The question should be, why wouldn't I? I've spent my entire life waiting for a man like you. What's another ten minutes or so?"

Kevin knew a come-on when he heard it. He also knew Valerie used flattery to get what she wanted. He wondered exactly what she wanted from him.

He moved away from her and circled his desk to sink into the plush office chair, where he leaned back and studied his lovely visitor. "Let's see if I can guess. Daddy gave you an assignment you don't like, and you want me to take it."

"Of course not." Her large blue eyes widened in mock horror. "I would never do such a thing."

Kevin chuckled. "How about the Anderson account?"

"Jim Anderson is a dirty, old man—literally and. . . and. . .well, you know." The look of disgust on her face stopped Kevin's mirth.

"I'm sorry, Valerie. That wasn't fair." He remembered how frightened she'd been when she came to him and told him what had happened when Mr. Anderson asked her to stop by for some tax receipts. She hadn't gone back, Kevin had seen to that. And she'd made him promise not to tell her father. The Anderson account was one of their larger ones.

"So what is it you need this time, Valerie?" Kevin gave her an encouraging smile and hoped he wouldn't have to run interference for her again.

"Something fun." Her eyes sparkled as she turned a bright smile on him and leaned one hip against his desk. "I know you like parties."

Kevin spoke before she could continue. "I'll be out of town next week. Leaving tomorrow and won't be back until Thursday. When's your party?"

She folded her arms across her chest with a *humph* followed by a sigh. "This Saturday night."

He shrugged. "Sorry."

She stood and faced him, the hint of a smile curving her lips. "You know you're my first choice, don't you?"

When he didn't speak, she said, "I'll find someone else who will be glad to take me. Think of that while you're all by your lonesome in some motel room."

She sashayed out the door, wiggling her fingers over her shoulder. "Bye, Kevin."

When the door clicked shut behind her, Kevin reached for his phone. A couple of rings later, a man answered, and he said, "Hi, this is Kevin Nichols. Is Trey there?"

"I'm sorry, he isn't. Can I take a message?" Kevin recognized Trey's dad's voice.

"Sure. I talked to Trey about going to a White Sox game. I've got tickets for the sixteenth. I'd like for all three of you to be my guests."

"Now that sounds like an idea." Mr. Miller's voice boomed. "I'll ask Mavis and Trey. And just between you and me, I'm expecting a yes."

Kevin laughed with him. "I sure hope so. Let me give you my cell phone number so you can reach me at any time. I'm looking forward to seeing you all again."

That evening Kevin packed for his trip and carried his suitcase into the living room and set it by the door. He turned to go back to his bedroom when he saw the Bible Trey had given him. The book sat alone on the lamp table beside his recliner, where a visitor might think he'd been reading it. But the truth was he hadn't opened his Bible since the Sunday morning he followed Sarah to church.

Guilt sat heavy in his chest, as he reached for the only gift his son had ever given him. That alone made the book valuable, but on some level deep inside, he knew the Bible represented much more than just a book. His parents had not attended church regularly, but they'd taught him to respect the Holy Bible. He held Trey's gift in his hands and a longing to discover its truths stole into his heart. He hadn't promised Trey he would read it, but he promised himself he would read a little tonight. And he would read more in the nights to come. Feeling as if his journey had already started, Kevin carried the Bible to his bedroom and placed it on his pillow as his cell phone rang.

He flipped it open. "Hello."

"Yeah, this is Trey. Dad said you invited us to a White Sox game?"

They talked for several minutes, setting up the time and place to meet. Somehow, talking to Trey seemed normal. Kevin hadn't looked forward to an outing so much in years.

eight

•

"Here's the pitch!" The announcer informed them of every move in the diamond below. They had a good view from the upper level near first base and were already at the bottom of the seventh inning.

Mrs. Miller leaned forward past Trey and spoke to Kevin, who sat next to the aisle. "I know we already said thank you, but this is a great outing for us." She laughed. "Okay, maybe just for me. I must admit I'm a baseball fan. You can have football, but I do enjoy a good baseball game."

Kevin grinned at Trey's mother. "I played football in high school and college, but I always played baseball during the summer."

"Trey likes his football, too." She smiled. "Maybe he got that from you."

Kevin met the open acceptance in her eyes and marveled. Trey's parents had been generous with their son from the start, when he asked them to stay in touch with him. And they'd kept their promise, sending him a letter and a current picture each year near Trey's birthday.

He'd been thrilled when they invited him to meet Trey a month ago, in March. He knew they'd invite Sarah, too, but he hadn't expected to become friends with her again. If their tentative relationship could be called friendship. He wasn't sure. Their few meetings had been great; still he feared the next one as much as he had the first.

Sarah held a part of his heart. Always had, always would. If he could do something to fix the problem with her home, he might not feel so unsure of her. Maybe he'd even ask her out again. Their last outing had been better than he'd expected, which was probably what scared him so much.

The crack of ball against bat brought the crowd to their feet. The announcer's voice yelling over the cheers added to the excitement. "There's the home run we've been waiting for."

The roar of the spectators, the loudspeaker, the whistles and calls became background to Kevin when he saw a woman jumping and shouting, her long blond ponytail swinging with her movement. Nothing could have taken him back in time quicker.

She was across the aisle, three seats over and probably six or seven rows down in front. He watched as Sarah leaned across a little girl and gave the man in the end seat a hug. His heart dipped to his stomach.

"Isn't that Sarah?" Trey's question as they resumed their seats told Kevin he hadn't dreamed her up. He'd seen her hug another man.

For a while she looked like the teenage girl he remembered. For just a moment she had been his again. But Sarah wasn't his. If nothing else impressed him of that fact, seeing her with another man had.

He gave Trey a quick grin to let him know he didn't mind seeing Sarah in another man's arms. "Yeah, looks like she had the same idea we did. Imagine that."

Forty thousand people crowded into a stadium this size, and he had to pick seats within sight of Sarah. What were the odds? He thought back to their school days and mentally shrugged. Okay, so maybe the odds were better than one might think. Sarah had always sat on the first base side to watch his games. Because he excelled at catching, he played either catcher or first baseman. She said she could see him better from the right side of the field no matter which position he played. Had he subconsciously chosen these seats because of their past? Had she?

"You are coming with us for something to eat after the game, aren't you?" Trey watched him closely, as if he truly wanted him to come.

Kevin thrilled at Trey's desire for them to develop a friendship, if nothing more. He could have carried resentment toward both him and Sarah, but amazingly he seemed to carry no excess baggage, and Kevin credited the Millers' parenting skills.

Now he nodded at Trey and smiled. "Sure, I wouldn't miss it."

A flicker of emotion crossed Trey's expression as he looked back toward Sarah. Still watching her, he asked, "Would you mind too much if I invite Sarah to join us?"

Trey's question hit Kevin's midsection with a healthy punch. Would he mind? Sarah, no. Her friend, yes.

"No, of course I don't mind. That would be great. Give you a chance to spend a little time getting to know her." Kevin kept his voice upbeat while he cringed at the thought of getting to know Sarah's friend. And who did the little girl belong to? She seemed to know Sarah pretty well, from the way they had their heads together. He watched Sarah point toward the outfield while the little girl nodded.

He turned back to Trey. "Looks like she's with someone. They might not want to let her go."

Trey brushed off his excuse for what it was. "That's okay. We'll invite them all."

He turned to his parents and talked to them for a few minutes then turned back to Kevin. "I think I'll go invite them. There's only a couple of more innings, and we don't want them lost in the crowd after the game."

"All right." Kevin stood to let Trey out. He folded back into his seat as if the air had been let out of his body. If he could keep Trey to himself he would, although he didn't mind sharing with Sarah. What he didn't like was sharing Sarah with some other guy and a kid.

He watched Trey stop at the end of the seats where Sarah sat. She turned when he called her name, and Kevin saw her eyes grow wide just before she leapt to her feet and reached for him.

"Trey." Her excited voice carried back to him, probably because he was so tuned in to her. She scooted past the little girl and leaned in front of the man to give Trey a quick but tight hug.

They talked for a bit, and he motioned toward his parents and Kevin. Sarah glanced up the aisle, and Kevin knew the moment she spotted him. The smile froze on her face. But she quickly recovered and introduced Trey to her friends. The man shook hands with him, they talked another couple of seconds, and then Trey strode back up the aisle.

Kevin stood again and let him in. Sarah watched before she sat back down. "So will she join us?"

Trey shot him a quick glance and nodded. "Yeah, she's with a doctor from the hospital where she works. The little girl is his. They all thought food sounded like a good idea. She gave me her cell phone number and said they'd meet us at the restaurant. I hope that's okay."

"Sure, it's fine."

Trey turned to tell his parents what Sarah had said, and Kevin didn't even try to pretend any more interest in the game. All he could see was Sarah. All he could think about was Sarah seemed much too familiar with her doctor friend and his little girl. A man like that probably had marriage on the brain. And why not? Sarah would make a wonderful wife, and from the way she and the little girl appeared to be getting along, she'd make a wonderful mother.

❧

Sarah saw Kevin emerge from his car as Harold pulled to a stop in the restaurant parking lot. She took a deep breath, knowing the next several minutes would be tense but not wanting to do or say anything to hurt Trey. She slipped from the car and watched Kevin cross the parking lot with Trey and his parents.

Her heart pounded with anticipation. Had he thought of her since the Friday night they'd gone out? She'd thought of little else, wondering if he'd call or stop by. He hadn't. She glanced at Harold. He hadn't wanted to join Trey's family but had done it for her. He was a good friend.

So was Katie. She smiled at the little girl, who climbed from the backseat. "You know, I'm really hungry. Too bad they don't have pizza here."

That earned her a big smile. "Me, too."

"Cheering uses a lot of energy, doesn't it?"

Katie nodded. "Yeah."

"Looks like we got here at the same time." Kevin and Trey stopped by Sarah and Katie.

Harold circled the car and touched Sarah's shoulder. He shook hands with Kevin. "I'm Doctor Jenson. Harold Jenson. Sarah's—"

"I'm sorry. I should have introduced you." Sarah felt heat rise in her face. What had Harold almost said? "Harold and I work at the same hospital, only he does the very important work of helping children get well."

She put her arm around Katie's shoulders and pulled her close. "This young lady is Katie Jenson. Judging from the story she wrote for her history class, I wouldn't be surprised if she grows up to be a writer." Sarah smiled down at Katie's beaming face, then up into Kevin's narrowed eyes.

What was wrong with him? She sighed silently. "Harold, Katie, I'd like for you to meet Kevin Nichols. Kevin is. . ." As her voice faltered, she resisted the urge to roll her eyes. Now she sounded like Harold. She'd been about to say Trey's father, but that would've been as bad as saying he was the love of her life. Either would be much too close to the truth and very inappropriate. She settled for saying, "Kevin is an accountant."

"A hungry accountant." Kevin smiled at Katie. "How about you, young lady? Are you ready to eat?"

Katie gave him a shy smile, bringing a frown of disapproval from her father. Harold touched Sarah's back, guiding her toward the restaurant.

Trey fell into step beside her, and she couldn't help pretending he was her son in every way. If she could go back in time, would she fight harder to keep him? She honestly didn't know. Seeing the wonderful young man he'd become reaffirmed she'd made the best decision. She smiled at him as they entered the restaurant and received a sweet smile in return.

"Thank you for inviting me."

His smile widened. "I talked with my mom and dad. They're okay with it. I mean, no offense, but they'll always be Mom and Dad to me. But I've got a lot of questions. The only thing is, I don't have the words to ask them. Does that make sense?"

Sarah sensed Kevin listening to every word she and Trey said.

She let Harold lead her to a table and hold her chair then take the one next to her. When Trey sat across the corner from her and Kevin slid into the seat beside him, Sarah finally answered Trey's question.

"Yes, it makes perfect sense. If you ever find those words, I'll do my best to answer—if I can." Her quick laugh brought a smile to both Trey and Kevin. Mrs. Miller glanced their way as she and her husband took the chairs across from Kevin and Trey.

Sarah had plenty of unanswered questions herself. At the home she had watched girls give their babies up for adoption, and most had no knowledge of the adoptive parents. She had seen the anguish some of the girls suffered because they knew they would never see their babies again.

She wondered which was better for all concerned, open or closed adoption. She could scarcely keep from watching Trey. She wanted to absorb and commit to memory the image of the young man her baby had become. She'd carried him for nine months. She'd had him with her that first day of his life until the Millers arrived to take him. Even then they allowed her to hold him and kiss him good-bye. But he was no longer her son. Trey Miller was the son of Tom and Mavis Miller. No matter how willing they were to share him, he was still their son. That truth brought bittersweet pain to her heart.

Kevin's voice cut into her musings. "The question I want answered is, which do you think is best? Chicken fried steak or crispy golden fried chicken?"

Sarah glanced up to meet Kevin's gaze, and he winked. Heat rose in her cheeks.

"The steak sounds good to me with a baked potato," Trey told the waitress.

After they gave their order, Kevin began talking with Tom about the game. Trey chimed in, and so did Mavis. Even Harold joined their conversation while Sarah listened. She didn't care about baseball. She'd only gone because it sounded like a fun outing.

Their talk of scores, batting averages, and who would be in the World Series went over her head. Kevin and Trey both glanced her way at different times as if to include her. She watched their dimples flash when they smiled and marveled at how much alike they were. Trey's name might be Miller, but he had a lot of Nichols in him, too.

Then she saw Tom gesture with his hands while he talked and noticed Trey doing the same thing. Their food came, and Mr. Miller prayed a short prayer. The conversation continued and drifted to Trey's graduation.

"It's at seven on Saturday, May 21st." Trey looked from Sarah to Kevin while a frown creased his forehead. "I hope you both can come. It's a two-hour drive."

"Don't worry." Kevin spoke before Sarah could. "We'll be there."

Sarah lifted her eyebrows at Kevin, but what could she say when he was right? She smiled at Trey. "Two hours isn't far. Of course I'll be there. I wouldn't miss your graduation. What would you like for a gift?"

A twinkle sparkled from his eyes as he grinned. "A new car."

"Trey Miller." His mother gasped, and everyone else laughed.

"Just kidding." He grinned at his mom. "Gotcha."

She looked like she didn't know whether to laugh or to scold him.

His eyes still twinkled when he turned back to Sarah. "I'm sorry, Sarah. I really was joking. I'm saving for a car, and I'll have one before I go to college. Really, you don't have to get me a gift at all. I only want you to come."

"Oh, we'll be there, and we'll think of something nice as a gift. You can't deny us that pleasure." Until Sarah looked up and saw the smile on Kevin's face, she didn't realize she'd included him.

Harold obviously noticed. He pushed his chair back and patted his stomach. "Well, now that's settled, Sarah, don't you think we should be going? We've got a pretty tired little girl here."

"Of course." Sarah looked at Katie, who had been so quiet, she'd all but forgotten her. As much as Katie liked being the center of attention, she'd probably been bored by the adult conversation.

"We need to go, too." Mrs. Miller said. "It's a long drive home, although we've enjoyed today a great deal."

Scarcely more than crumbs remained as everyone shoved their chairs back and prepared to leave. In the parking lot, Trey stopped Sarah and Kevin, while his parents went ahead. Harold paused then turned away to help his daughter into his car.

"I just want you to know how glad I am I got to meet you. I've known about you all my life. I mean writing those letters on my birthday and all. But you weren't real to me until we met." He looked from one to the other. "You were always included in my bedtime prayers when I was little. That was Mom's idea, but now that I know you, it's my idea. I'm praying for you, and well, I'd appreciate your prayers for me, too."

Sarah saw the serious expression on Kevin's face and wondered if he resented the implication that he needed prayer. She did. Only Trey's request for their prayers softened her heart.

Kevin spoke first. "I've been reading the Bible you gave me. I never read it much before, and I'm finding it a lot more interesting than I thought."

"Yeah, it's pretty awesome." Trey nodded. "If you listen down deep inside, God will speak to you through your Bible reading. That's just one of the joys of being a Christian."

Sarah smiled and nodded as if she knew what he meant. She'd gone to church all her life. She accepted Christ as a child and still attended church even after moving away from her parents' influence. Surely that counted for something.

"Sarah, are you ready to go?" Harold stood a few feet away waiting.

"Yes, of course." She gave Trey a quick hug and kiss on the cheek. "Thank you, Trey, for letting us know you better. Don't forget to send your graduation announcement. I'm looking forward to it."

He grinned. "Me, too."

"I'll bet," Kevin said.

&

Kevin watched Sarah walk away with her doctor boyfriend. His heart felt as if a rock weighed it down. He'd been within arm's length of her most of the evening and hadn't touched her once.

Why had it come as a surprise to see her with another man? Did he really think she would wait eighteen years for him to show up and with one word of apology win her love again? He couldn't help wondering why she'd never married. With her looks, her personality, sweetness, intelligence. . . He could go on and on, but the truth was, Sarah could have any man she wanted. He'd always known that and marveled that she once wanted him.

He took the Millers to his apartment, where their car waited. Tom declined his invitation to go inside. "No, we need to get home. It's been a long day. Maybe we can get together another time."

"That sounds good." Kevin liked the Millers, and he especially craved time with Trey, but all at once, he couldn't wait for them to leave.

He wanted to see Sarah again. Only this time he wanted her all to himself with no distractions. She and Trey had talked about questions. Well, he had a few of his own. He'd like to know what Sarah thought of Trey and of him. But even more, he wanted to know what her intentions were toward that doctor. They'd looked too much like a cozy little family for his peace of mind.

Half an hour later Kevin pulled onto Sarah's street. He drove past her house and saw the doctor's car sitting in her driveway. What did he do? Take his little girl to her house for a nap? Didn't the guy know when to leave?

Kevin circled the cul-de-sac and went home.

&

Monday, Kevin called Sarah's hospital. He reached her office but was told she wasn't in. He didn't leave a message or his name.

On Tuesday morning, Kevin made a special trip to the hospital and to the personnel office. A woman in the outer office smiled at him. "Hello, may I help you?"

"Yes, I need to speak with Sarah Maddox."

The woman's tag said Tricia Simmons. She met his gaze. "I'm sorry, but she isn't in right now."

"This is her office, isn't it?"

"Yes, it is." Tricia pulled a pad of paper toward her. "Would you like to leave a message?"

"Not really." Kevin stifled a sigh of frustration. "Just tell her Kevin Nichols stopped by."

"Kevin Nichols?" Tricia's eyes lit up, and she shoved the paper away. "She's in the oncology ward with the children right now. Why don't you see if you can find her?"

As Tricia gave him directions, he wondered at the change in her attitude but soon forgot to care as he headed toward Sarah.

A few minutes later, he stopped outside a doorway and watched a Sarah he scarcely recognized. Dressed in a clown costume that looked like a garish grandmother with multicolored hair, Sarah moved from one child to another giving hugs and listening to the childish chatter.

While he watched, she picked up a small child and sat on a chair with her held close in her arms. All the love he had ever felt for Sarah, and more besides, swept through his heart until he felt as if he might weep. Without catching the attention of anyone in the room, he turned away.

He walked through the halls to the entrance and outside, scarcely noticing his surroundings. What had just happened? He wanted Sarah to forgive him for the past. He owed her that much and more. But love? Why hadn't he known being near her again would cause him to fall in love with her just as he had when they were teenagers? Yet how could he bear it if she turned from him as she had done before? How could he risk losing Sarah twice?

nine

Sarah waited until the other board members left Marilee's Home before she poured tea for herself and lifted questioning brows toward her friend. "How about a refill?"

Darlene nodded and held out her glass. "What do you think, Sarah? Will it work?"

"A fund-raising banquet?" Sarah poured the tea and set it in front of Darlene before she resumed her place across the table. Nothing they did would ever be enough, but Sarah couldn't say that. The board agreed a banquet would raise the most money in the short time they had, and their attitudes had been positive. One businessman even donated the use of his banquet facilities.

She adopted that same positive spirit and said, "Why not? We'll work hard and make it work. I've got a list of names to call. Past contributors are likely to come, or at the very least, send a good donation, don't you think?"

"But less than a month?" Darlene shuddered and took a sip of tea. "How on earth will we get everything done?"

Sarah shrugged, not wanting to admit she had doubts, too. "Delegation. Everyone has a part. Get the girls to help. This affects them the most. If you can get one or two of the graduates to speak, that will be wonderful. We should look for another location, too."

"What happened to your friend? Mr. Nichols." Darlene lifted hopeful eyes toward Sarah, who almost snorted.

"My friend, you say? I sometimes wonder."

"But that day you brought him here, I heard him say he'd see what he could do."

Sarah released an audible sigh. "I know. I'm sorry, Darlene. I tried to show him what we're doing. I thought he sympathized, but I stopped asking when he so neatly avoided the subject."

"Are you still seeing him?" Darlene sounded hesitant, as if she were afraid to ask.

Sarah gave a quick laugh. "You make it sound like we're dating. Actually, I've been seeing a very nice doctor."

"Dr. Jenson." Darlene smiled. "He isn't as good-looking as Mr. Nichols, but you're right. He's very nice. So are things getting serious?"

Sarah laughed. "He wishes."

She stayed another half an hour chatting with Darlene while they straightened the dining room and kitchen before she went home.

❧

Sarah whittled her list of contributors by calling as many as she could reach during the evening. She put calls in to the business numbers from her office, squeezing a call here and there around her duties at work.

Everyone she'd called seemed concerned. Now if only they put their concern into action.

She had time for one more call. A receptionist answered, "Parker Enterprises. May I help you?"

"Yes, Mr. John Parker, please." Sarah waited while her call was transferred.

❧

Kevin figured he walked past Mr. Parker's office at the wrong time when Valerie stuck her head out the door and motioned to him. "*Pssst*, Kevin. Come here."

He tried to imitate a tough guy pose. "Sure, doll, whataya need?"

"Oh, stop that and get in here." She motioned frantically.

He shrugged. "You're the boss's daughter."

She grabbed his arm and pulled him the rest of the way into

the room. "Yes, and if you want me to stay the boss's daughter, you'd better help me."

"Hey, it's what I do best." Kevin stopped her from closing the door all the way. "But the door stays open."

"Oh all right, just don't let Daddy know I messed up." She circled the room and plopped into her father's desk chair, then motioned for Kevin to take another chair she pulled up beside her. "Sit down and help me with this."

"And this would be?" Kevin sat where he was told.

"I just did this guy's taxes, now he wants me to straighten out his bookkeeping for this year. Last year's was bad enough."

"And the problem is?" Kevin looked at the neat columns of figures and frowned. What was Valerie up to?

She turned two large brown eyes toward him and whispered, "I can't get this to balance. I keep getting different totals."

"Valerie, this looks pretty good to me. Why are you—"

"That's my writing, Kevin. Of course it looks good."

"Your writing?" He stared at her. "Why aren't you using a program? You know we use computers now."

Her chin lifted in a defiant tilt. "Because I thought it would be easier this way. Look at this."

She snatched up a shoe box and shoved it at him. Inside were receipts and torn pieces of paper covered with scribbling. Thankfully he hadn't seen such a mess in years. He whistled. "Daddy doesn't play favorites, does he?"

"No, he doesn't." Her voice caught, and Kevin felt the stirrings of compassion begin when the phone rang.

"Would you get that?" She jumped up and headed toward the door. "I'll be right back."

Kevin lifted the receiver. "John Parker's office. Th—"

The caller cut him off before he could give his name. "Mr. Parker, this is Sarah Maddox. I represent Merilee's Home, which is a home for young girls who desperately need our help. Many girls have turned their lives and the lives of their babies around through the efforts of this work, and now their home is being threatened. In approximately two months, wreckers will begin to tear down the building where they live. You have contributed before to this worthy cause, and we are asking you to again dig deep to help these girls. On Saturday evening, May fourteenth, we will be holding a fund-raising banquet to help pay for the move being forced on those who live in Marilee's Home."

Kevin leaned back in Parker's chair and listened to Sarah's voice as she gave her spiel to the wrong man. Should he set her straight? Naw, why bother? She'd just blame him for interfering.

"So can we count on you and your wife attending the banquet?" Sarah finally ran down and waited for his answer.

Keeping it short, Kevin deepened his voice so she wouldn't recognize him. "I'll do my best."

"Some who are unable to attend have promised a donation. Of course we would much prefer meeting you in person and giving you the opportunity to hear of the successes of our work, but anything you can do will be greatly appreciated." She sounded desperate.

"I'll keep that in mind. Thanks." Kevin hung up before he said something that would give him away. He had the time and place written down. Now he'd make a note for Mr. Parker.

Valerie slipped through the door just as he stuck the note on top of the pile on his boss's desk. "Was that call important?"

He grinned at her. "Not another job if that's what you're worried about. Just someone wanting a contribution."

❧

When Sarah opened the door two weeks later to a bouquet of roses and Harold's best smile, she should have known something was up. When he took her to Willis Tower Skydeck, where they could look down at the beautiful lights of the city set against the black night, she should have slipped away and called a cab. But she didn't. Instead she fell into the mood he created. After all, she didn't get dressed up and go out on the town every night. She liked being pursued, and Harold had pursuing down to an art.

Then the waiter brought dessert. Cheesecake chimichanga and chocolate pudding.

"Oh Harold, I don't know if I can eat another thing." Sarah spread her fingers across her waist for emphasis.

He smiled at her. "This has no calories and it's very good. I know you like chocolate. Try some for me."

Harold had impeccable manners, so Sarah's eyes widened when he reached across the table and picked up her fork. He dipped it in her pudding and held the offering in front of her mouth. "Here, just take this at least."

Sarah pulled back. "There's something on the end of the fork."

When Harold didn't move but continued to watch her, she looked at the fork again. How could something have gotten into dessert here? It looked metal, like someone's ring caught on the end of her fork. No, that couldn't happen. She lifted her gaze back to Harold's.

He looked into her eyes. "Sarah, take it from the fork. Please say yes."

"Yes?" Her throat constricted. What did he mean? She plucked the ring from its bed of chocolate and dropped it on her napkin. She quickly wiped her fingers and the ring, then left it lying on the napkin and clasped her trembling hands in her lap.

The white gold ring sported a cluster of diamonds with two small diamonds on either side. Sarah stared at it as if it might crawl to the edge of the table and fall into her hands, or even worse, slide onto her finger. Third finger, left hand. An engagement ring. Why hadn't she seen this coming? Even more important, what should she do about Harold and his ring? She made the mistake of looking at him and reading the uncertainty in his eyes.

"Oh Harold." She barely choked out those two words.

He placed the fork on her plate. "Don't make a decision now. I took you by surprise. I thought the way you and Katie were getting along. . . You're good for her, Sarah. Will you do me a favor?"

She nodded, just becoming aware other diners had picked up on the drama unfolding at their table. The waiter, hovering in the area, turned and walked away as if he were disappointed. How could she not do whatever Harold asked after spoiling his wonderful proposal?

"Will you please take the ring home with you and keep it until you know for sure what your answer is?" He slipped a jeweler's box across the table.

She nodded and nestled the ring into its red velvet bed, snapped the box closed, and dropped it into her purse. As if by mutual agreement, Sarah and Harold rose and left their uneaten cheesecake sitting on the table.

Several minutes later, Harold walked Sarah to her door, and she lifted her lips for a chaste kiss, then turned and went inside alone. She watched through the living room window as Harold returned to his car, but she saw Kevin in her mind, and her heart felt as if it might break into a million pieces.

She turned from the window, dug the ring box from her handbag, tossed it on the coffee table, and hurried from the room.

❧

One week later, Kevin drove home from a business trip with barely enough time to shower and dress for Sarah's banquet. He whistled a tune as he jogged toward his car. The convention hall's lot was nearly full. He hoped that meant the home would reach their goal.

A young girl handed him a program at the door and took

his sizeable donation. Another escorted him to one of many small tables covered with white linen. A vase of flowers adorned the center of each table. He would have preferred sitting with Sarah, but he sat in the remaining chair and spoke to his dinner companions, a single woman and an older couple who looked to be in their fifties. They said they'd helped get Marilee's Home started twenty years ago.

"They've done a lot of good for these girls." The woman glanced across the room.

Kevin followed her gaze and saw Sarah talking with a young woman. As he watched, she moved to a center table and stood behind it, waiting until the buzz of conversation in the room grew quiet. "Good evening. I'm Sarah Maddox, chairman of the board at Marilee's Home. I'd like to welcome you tonight and thank you for coming. Reverend Beam from St. Paul's Community Church has graciously consented to offer the blessing over our food."

A tall gray-haired man stood, and Kevin bowed his head with everyone else while the man prayed. After that, waitresses wheeled carts to the tables and put plates in front of each guest. Thinly sliced beef roast smothered in brown gravy dominated the meal with creamy mashed potatoes and green beans nestled to the side. The enticing aroma stirred Kevin's appetite, until he noticed Sarah's dinner companion.

The possessive Dr. Jenson had somehow weaseled his way into the chair beside her. Kevin refused to let the stuffed shirt across the room ruin his enjoyment of the evening, however. He cut a small section of meat and turned his attention to his food and Mrs. Burns, the single lady beside him who could probably keep the conversation going without any help. In fact, between her and the other lady, Kevin figured his nod and occasional smile convinced them he listened.

Truthfully, he paid little attention to them, and he scarcely listened to the speeches following dinner. Even Sarah's speech didn't impress him nearly as much as watching the animation on her face and the movement of her lips while she talked. He figured he could watch Sarah and listen to the sound of her voice all night without growing bored. He tried to compare her with Valerie Parker and came up empty. There could be no comparison of two women who were so different. Besides, he didn't want to think of Valerie. She had been seeking him out more each week, almost as if she was pursuing him. He blocked her from his mind and focused on Sarah. Then Sarah sat down, and the young woman she'd been talking to before dinner stood in her place.

"Hi, I'm Kaitlin Rosaro, and I'm a former resident of Marilee's Home." She went on to tell the familiar story of a teenage girl who thought she was in love. "But he didn't love me." Her dark brown eyes clouded as she spoke. "When I told him, he said he couldn't take care of a wife and a baby. He walked away while I took the responsibility for our mistake. Maybe I could have made it if I'd had the support of a family, but my mom died when I was twelve. My dad never stayed home. I thought about getting rid of the baby, but I couldn't. When my dad found out, he got mad. To make a long story short, he kicked me out of the house. I stayed with friends. A night here and a night there until their folks got tired of too many overnights. That's when I heard about Marilee's Home. I applied for the program and moved in within a couple of days."

Kaitlin continued her story, telling how she finished high school at Marilee's Home while she worked part-time. Of how she'd gone on to college and now worked as a high school counselor, trying to help other girls avoid the mistakes she had made. For the first time that evening, Kevin listened, really listened to one of the speakers. He listened to Kaitlin, but he thought of Sarah. What would she have done if her parents had kicked her out after he walked away? Only he hadn't walked away until she got angry and refused to speak to him. Then he'd let his parents pressure him into turning away from Sarah. He'd even dated other girls, while Sarah grew big with the burden of their son. Remorse for his unconcern swept over him, as he finally understood why Marilee's Home was so important to Sarah.

Love for the wonderful woman Sarah had become filled Kevin's heart, and he knew he had to see her again soon. More than anything he wanted to spend time with her, be with her, and listen to her talk. Watch her smile. Feel her happiness. Experience the inner joining of their spirits as their love returned and grew beyond the limitations of their youth.

The program ended and Kevin stood. He shook hands with those at his table, eager to get to Sarah's side. As soon as possible, he hurried to the head table where Sarah stood talking to a couple of women. Her boyfriend stood so close to her, they almost touched. The doctor thought he had a prior claim on Sarah? Too bad. Kevin waited until the women turned away, then he stepped forward.

"Good program, Sarah." He ignored the doctor.

"Kevin." Her eyes lit up for a moment. "I didn't expect to see you here."

"Oh, really?" He smiled. "I received a special invitation and couldn't resist."

"How nice."

He loved watching the confusion in her beautiful blue eyes. "Yes, a lovely lady called me at Parker Enterprises. Of course, she called me Mr. Parker, but I know she wanted me to come. Don't you think so, Sarah?"

Kevin knew the second Sarah understood from the expression in her eyes. "That was you on the phone? Why didn't you tell me?"

He laughed. "I tried. You kept talking, so I kept quiet."

"But Mr. Parker is one of our larger contributors." Her voice rose.

Kevin nodded toward the far side of the room. "Don't worry, he's here. I'm sure he made a good-sized donation."

Dr. Jenson had been quietly waiting. Now he slipped his hand around Sarah's waist and spoke. "Is there anything we should be doing, Sarah?"

Before she could answer, Kevin said, "Oh don't mind me. I'm leaving." He regained Sarah's attention. "Tomorrow night we're going out on the town. Wear old clothes. Blue jeans and a T-shirt would be perfect."

He could have sworn under oath he saw smoke rise from Jenson's ears. Just to make sure, he added, "This fascination you've developed for the Mother Road is catching. You know there's a bike trail on the old road. I've lived along Route 66 all my life and pretty well ignored it. Now I'm finding there's more to the road than I ever knew."

Kevin smirked at the doctor before giving Sarah a wink. "Yep, a bike ride at night on the Mother Road should satisfy those romantic notions you get. Be ready at seven."

He didn't give either of them a chance to respond as he turned and walked out of the meeting room.

ten

Sarah pulled her oldest T-shirt over her head and let it fall to the outside of her equally worn blue jeans. Kevin wanted old, so that's what he'd get. She brushed her hair up into a ponytail and secured it with an elastic holder then laughed at her reflection in the mirror. If she owned a bicycle, she'd make Kevin eat his words and take her riding. She was certainly dressed for it.

What could he have planned? Harold had thrown a fit after Kevin left last night. He'd threatened to spend the evening with her so he could protect her from that lunatic. Only he couldn't because he had to leave town for a seminar. Didn't she know how dangerous bike riding in the city was and especially at night? He'd gone on and on until she finally convinced him Kevin had no intention of biking. He'd only been goading Harold. And had he ever succeeded.

With a pointed reminder that his engagement ring was still in her possession, Harold said she shouldn't be dating other men. But she wasn't dating Kevin. Not really. Besides, she offered to give the ring back, and he refused to take it. He said she needed more time to get her priorities straight. The ring still sat on her coffee table closed up in its box because Sarah was afraid of hurting Harold's feelings. Soon, she reminded herself, she would have to.

Her doorbell rang. She hurried to the door and peeked through the security viewer. One hand pulled the door open while the other splayed across her abdomen in an attempt to quiet the butterflies fluttering inside. His faded blue jeans had a frayed hole in the knee. He wore a blue denim jacket over a white T-shirt, and his dark hair looked windblown and touchable. Dimples deepened in a smile just for her. Somehow he'd become the boy she remembered, and she swayed with the impact of emotions she couldn't handle. She grabbed her jacket and draped it over her shoulder as she blinked, forcing her mind to the present.

"So where are the bikes?" She stepped out on the porch with him and closed the door.

"Bikes?" His grin widened. "We can't ride bikes at night in Chicago, Sarah. There's too much traffic. We'll enjoy Route 66 from the car. You ready?"

"Sure." She fell into step beside him and didn't resist when his fingers touched hers and slipped together in the familiar hold from their youth. Harold always guided her with a hand at her waist. She liked holding hands with Kevin.

He held her door then walked around and took his place behind the wheel before asking, "Have you ever been to Lou Mitchell's?"

"Yes, hasn't everyone?"

"Um, no. Is it a good place to eat?"

"Kevin, Lou Mitchell's is one of the original restaurants on Route 66. Of course it's a good place to eat."

He grinned at her. "Too bad, 'cause we aren't going there. They closed at three."

She fought the urge to laugh with him. "Where are you taking me, then?"

He turned the corner and entered the busy street. "I should let you guess, but we're going to Henry's Drive-In for a hot dog. I've heard they're well worth the drive."

"You've never been there, either, have you?" She gave him a stern look. "I'll bet you don't go anywhere that isn't sit-down service with a waiter. What happened to the down-home boy I used to know?"

His expression as he turned toward her conveyed a depth

of feeling that had her heart pounding. "I'm here, Sarah. Just older and a bit jaded. But I still appreciate what's important, and I know what I want."

"What do you want, Kevin?" As soon as the words left her mouth, she regretted them. What if she didn't want to hear what he had to say?

"Right now?" He grinned. "I want a hot dog. How about you? Doesn't that sound good? But only one. I don't want you too full. You can have something to drink though."

Sarah laughed. "You're making no sense whatsoever."

He chuckled. "You'll see."

At Henry's Drive-In, Kevin ordered one hot dog, and they shared it, although he bought them each a soft drink. Sarah didn't question his motives. Kevin's surprises had always been fun.

His next stop was a miniature golf course.

"Oh, I haven't done this in ages." Sarah felt the years roll backward as they laughed together when Kevin's ball jumped over the hole instead of going in. They held hands and stood with shoulders touching, yet she felt a barrier. Something that kept them from getting too close emotionally. She couldn't cross the invisible line that had been drawn so long ago and strengthened by their disagreement over Marilee's Home.

She'd loved Kevin so much, but she'd hated him just as intensely for the last eighteen years. How could she forgive him for the past when she couldn't forgive herself? What they'd done was her fault as much as his. She thought their love and their promise to marry someday made everything all right. She knew better now.

"Last hole." Kevin caught her attention. "Let's see you get a high score on this one."

"Ha, ha. Not a chance." Sarah held her club against the ball, as she sighted the distance to the windmill and watched the blades sweep the ground in front of the hole. Just as a blade covered the hole, she hit her ball, sending it rolling toward the windmill. The blades rotated, leaving the little door in the windmill open, and her ball rolled through.

"A hole in one? 'I haven't done this in ages.'" Kevin mocked her while his eyes twinkled. He set his ball down. "I should just turn my ball in."

She laughed. "Want me to do it for you?"

He lifted his eyebrows. "Careful. Pride goeth before a fall."

"You've been reading the Bible." Sarah couldn't stop the surprise from sounding in her voice.

He shrugged. "Yeah, I told Trey I would. I assumed you had, too."

"I have. I do." Guilt made her tell the truth. "Okay, I've read a little, just not every day like he asked."

"I know." Kevin touched his ball with his club. "It's easy to forget, but really, reading a little each evening isn't much of a chore. Besides, once you get started it's pretty interesting. There's a lot of good stuff in there, and it seems to relate to real life." He grinned at her. "You know, like your prideful attitude."

"Oh, you." She slapped his arm just as he hit the ball.

"Hey!" He started to complain until his ball rolled through the windmill door and returned through the works to the miniature golf office. "I got a hole-in-one. Thanks, Sarah. Guess I needed your help after all."

"Admit you couldn't have done it without me," she teased him, and they argued all the way to the car.

After they left the golf course, Kevin drove east and north to Lake Shore Drive. The sun had already traveled low in the western sky when they parked at an unusually deserted stretch of beach and climbed from the car.

Sarah had never seen the ocean, but Lake Michigan stretched enormous beyond the horizon, just as she figured an ocean would. A lone sailboat far from shore looked small on the vast water sparkling with orange and white reflections against the deep blue depths.

They held hands as they walked slowly toward the water while their shoes sank in the sand. Their shadows fell before them in elongated imitation linked together with their joined hands. Kevin's voice sounded soft in the evening against a background of traffic and city noises. "I'm glad you came with me tonight."

"Me, too."

"Want to take your shoes off?" He stopped and waited for her answer.

She grinned and nodded. Harold would never go barefoot on a city beach. There might be broken glass. He would only think of the danger.

Kevin grinned. "I figured as much. Stuff your socks in your shoes and tie the laces together."

They slipped their shoes and socks off then strolled on down the beach with their shoes hanging over their shoulders.

"Tell me about your life." Kevin spoke after several minutes of silence. "Fill in the blanks for me."

When she hesitated, he said, "Please, Sarah. I want to know everything about you. Where did you go to college? Who were your friends? Did you plan to be a personnel director in a hospital? What have you done for the last eighteen years?"

They stopped and faced each other. He placed his hand over his chest. "I have a big empty feeling here. Please help me fill it with mental images of your life."

Sarah understood because she felt so empty at times, too. She stood holding Kevin's hand, but it wasn't enough. Something important was missing. Something to do with love and fulfillment. If anyone could fill her heart, she knew it must be Kevin.

"I wouldn't mind hearing about your life, too, Kevin."

The hint of a smile touched his lips. "Let's sit down here and watch that sailboat while we talk."

"Okay."

They talked while the sailboat drifted down the lake until it became a tiny speck. A couple strolled past, and a lone man walked by, but Kevin and Sarah scarcely noticed as they became acquainted all over again. Their shadows faded into the darkening evening before Kevin asked, "There's one thing I need to know, Sarah. Why did you never marry?"

She looked at him and read the uncertainty in his gaze. He really wanted to know, so she told him the truth. "I never found anyone I could love."

"Are you hungry?"

"What?" She laughed when he took her hands and pulled her to her feet. "How do we go from baring our souls to 'Are you hungry?'"

His grin took her breath as usual. "It's getting late. We need to get out of here before some ruffian decides to ask for a donation. Besides, my hot dog half is gone, and I have a special dinner planned."

In the car, she asked, "So where are we going?"

"I'll tell you when we get there." Kevin drove across town, expertly dodging her questions until she gave up.

"All right, but it'd better be good." She retied her athletic shoe. "Hopefully we'll have curbside service. Most restaurants frown at this much sand."

"Nope." He chuckled. "We'll be dining in tonight."

Sarah didn't much care where they ate as long as the evening didn't end too soon. This time with Kevin had brought her home in a way she hadn't expected. Where had the hatred gone? The hurt and bitterness she'd carried so long? She thought back over the past couple of months and couldn't put her finger on a time when she had stopped thinking of Kevin as the enemy. More and more her thoughts and feelings were returning to the way it had been so long ago.

When he turned into a parking lot and stopped, she turned quickly to look at him. "Why are we at your apartment?"

"Because we're hungry?" He answered with a question and an innocent look.

She frowned. "Kevin, I won't do—"

"Don't even say it, Sarah." He gripped the steering wheel. "I won't, either. But I see nothing wrong with us eating a meal I've prepared in my kitchen. Do you?"

She shook her head, her eyes downcast. He got out and circled the car to open her door. "I'm sorry, Kevin. I shouldn't have doubted you. You've been a perfect gentleman, and I had no cause."

"You're forgiven." He smiled, and they turned toward the door.

Maybe too much of a gentleman. Beyond holding hands, Kevin hadn't offered any indication he wanted more than friendship from her. Would a kiss be out of line? But he hadn't backed down from demolishing Marilee's Home. She wouldn't think of kisses until the girls were taken care of. They had to keep looking for a building. So far nothing they'd looked into had been acceptable.

When Kevin ushered her into his apartment, and she saw the table set for two with a bouquet of fresh flowers in the center and a candle on each end, she forgot the home and their differences.

"Let me get these warmed up, and then we'll eat." Kevin pulled some covered dishes from the refrigerator and placed one in the microwave. "This shouldn't take long. Why don't you sit at the table?"

Sarah stepped into his tiny kitchen instead. "Can I help? What do you have to drink?"

"Here." He opened the refrigerator again and pulled a plastic jug out. "Pour this in the glasses on the table."

"Mmm. Sweet tea. My favorite." Sarah took the jug from him and stepped around the bar separating his kitchen from the dining area. She looked into the open living room, dining, and kitchen areas, then turned to the table and poured tea. "You have a nice apartment. Very clean and neat for a bachelor."

"Small but not bad," he agreed. "I'm not here all the time, so I don't need much. As an accountant, I travel a lot."

"Sounds like an interesting job."

"It'll do." He grinned. "I like buying and selling old properties better."

"I wish you hadn't said that." Sarah frowned as she handed the tea to him.

His eyebrows rose. "I told you I was working on something for your girls. Don't you trust me?"

"Why should I trust the guy who kicked us out in the first place?"

He made a *tsk*ing sound with his tongue as he set a casserole dish on the table. "Are we going to fight when we have all this good food waiting?"

Sarah leaned forward to sniff the rising steam that smelled delicious and stirred her appetite. "What is this?"

"Shepherd's pie."

She glanced up. "With lamb?"

He laughed. "No, hamburger just like Mom taught me. Hope you like green beans."

"Mmm, yummy. All right, hurry and get the rest of it on the table so I can otherwise occupy my mouth."

He chuckled and turned as the conventional oven timer sounded. "There's the bread."

Golden brown home-cooked rolls joined the casserole on the table. Sarah sat in a chair and watched Kevin wipe his countertop. This was a side of him she'd never seen.

He looked so domestic. Too domestic.

"Don't tell me you actually made this bread."

He looked up with a grin. "Okay, I won't."

"It looks homemade."

"It is."

She held his gaze until he laughed. "All right. If you must know, the dough came frozen in little balls. All I did was set it out in a pan for a while and put it in the oven. I stuck it back in for a few minutes to warm. It should be pretty good."

"No doubt, but something tells me you could do the whole mixing and kneading bit if you tried." She laughed at the look on his face. "Then again, maybe not."

"You are right. Not." He joined her at the table. "It isn't much, but I didn't think we'd want a full-course meal after the hot dog. Besides, this was easy. Go ahead, see what you think."

Sarah reached for his hand. "I don't always pray before I eat, but after meeting Trey, I've felt like something's missing if I don't. Do you mind?"

His fingers closed around hers, and a warmth spread up her arm. "I don't mind. Do you want me to?"

At her nod, he began. "God, we appreciate all You give us, including our food tonight. We pray for Your blessing as we eat. In Jesus' name. Amen."

Sarah had never felt closer to Kevin than at that moment. The love she had fought so hard for the last several weeks unfurled in her heart. Finally she pulled her hand back and picked up her fork. How could she forget the girls? How could she so easily forgive Kevin?

After they ate, Sarah helped Kevin clean up. Their evening out on the town had come to an end. She couldn't remember when she'd had a better time. In Kevin's car, she leaned back and closed her eyes for a moment. Why couldn't tonight stretch on into tomorrow and the next day and the next?

"If you aren't too tired, I'd like to make one more stop." Kevin turned the key, bringing his car to life.

She smiled across at him. "No, I'm not tired. I've enjoyed tonight, Kevin. A lot. Thanks for taking me."

He stopped at the street and gave her an intense look. "It's been my pleasure."

She let her smile linger as they drove across the city toward her house. Then Kevin turned onto a side street, and she remembered he'd said there'd be one more stop. Surely he couldn't come up with anything better than what they'd already done.

When he slowed in an older residential area and pulled into the drive of a large two-story Victorian house, she sat up straighter. Did he plan to introduce her to someone?

"There aren't any lights." She peered through the window for a closer look. A black wrought-iron fence surrounded the front yard. The wide, covered porch welcomed them. The driveway continued back to an unattached two-car garage. She saw privacy fencing with a gate between the garage and the house.

When Kevin didn't move, she asked, "Who lives here?"

"No one now." He opened his door. "Let's take a quick look around."

Before she could object, he helped her from the car. "Come on, Sarah. I own this house."

"You? Why?" She didn't know what to ask, so she let him lead her through the privacy gate to the back door, which he opened with a key.

He turned the light on as they stepped into a spacious kitchen complete with stove, refrigerator, and dishwasher. From there they toured a walk-in pantry, a large dining room, living room, three bedrooms, and a full bathroom. Upstairs were four more bedrooms and another full bathroom. Wallpaper needed to be replaced in a couple of rooms, but the floors were solid.

Kevin stood in the doorway of the last bedroom upstairs and leaned against the wide frame. "Well, what do you think?"

Sarah tried to keep her face expressionless but knew she probably failed. This house would be perfect for Marilee's Home. Would Kevin show it to her and then jerk it away by saying he had another purpose in mind? Or asking more than they could afford to pay or rent?

"It's a grand old home, Kevin. My guess is some rich man built this house a hundred years ago."

"You're probably right, but I want to know if you can use it for your home."

"The other board members would have to see it, but I can't imagine why they wouldn't like this. It's better than what we have." She ran her hand along the dark carved wood door frame in a caressing motion. "Our problem would be the cost. We have a lot of overhead and not much income."

Kevin grinned. "I'm sure we can work something out."

He glanced into the hall. "I got this at a bargain, Sarah. I can afford to sell cheap, but I was thinking about making a donation instead. You can use your money from the banquet to redecorate and buy furniture."

When he turned back and met her gaze, Sarah didn't know what to do. Falling into his arms was not an option, although that was her first choice. She smiled at the eager yet hesitant look in his eyes and did exactly what she knew she shouldn't.

"Oh Kevin." She lifted her arms and took a step forward. "Thank you."

He met her halfway and enfolded her within his embrace. She was at home in his arms. His head lowered. Hers raised. The kiss she wanted, but shouldn't have, swept her into the past and the future at the same time. She'd never before experienced such intensity of love as she did at that moment.

eleven

Kevin woke early Sunday morning happier than he remembered being in a long time. When he threw the covers back and sat up, his hand hit his Bible. He'd gone to sleep reading from the Gospel of John and hadn't placed it on the table as he usually did. He picked the book up, an idea forming in his mind. Why not go to church?

Valerie and her father had been trying to get him to attend with them for the last several weeks. In fact, John asked again Friday when he left the office. He'd put them off, but today he wanted to go. Only not to the Parkers' church.

He glanced at the clock. Time for a shower and a quick breakfast before driving to Sarah's. He grinned as he padded barefoot to the bathroom. She would be surprised to see him. And glad, he hoped.

Several minutes later, he left his apartment and drove to Sarah's with his Bible on the seat beside him. She answered his knock almost immediately.

"Hey, you ready for church?"

She lifted her eyebrows. "I am, but what are you doing here?"

He grinned. "I felt like going to church today and hoped you wouldn't mind if I tag along with you."

"No, I don't mind at all." She still seemed bewildered, as if she thought he was joking. "Let me grab my Bible and purse."

She disappeared inside for less than a minute and returned with her white Bible held close. "Okay, I'm ready."

As the church came into view, Kevin asked, "Have you

been reading your Bible?"

"I did last night." Sarah gave him a sheepish smile. "I figured if you can, I can."

Kevin nodded. "Trey suggested I start reading in John. I skip around some, but lately I've been staying in the Gospels, learning about Jesus' life and His teachings."

"He told me to read in John, too." Sarah stared straight ahead. "I've always gone to church. I know the Bible, but I admit I haven't studied it like I should. Especially lately."

Kevin found a place to park on the lot next to the church. "The Gospel of John is about being born again. I memorized John 3:16 when I was a kid in Sunday school, but I never thought much about it until now."

He didn't know how to explain the conflicting emotions that churned in his heart when he thought about being born again. He didn't know if he was ready to change his life so drastically in order to make such a commitment. He still had a lot of reading to do, and a lot of thinking.

He walked with Sarah to the church and followed her to her usual seat just as the service began. The songs were nice—especially the short choruses of praise at the beginning. He didn't understand how, but all the voices lifted in praise set the mood for the rest of the service.

When the minister stood behind the pulpit and began speaking on the fifteenth chapter of John, Kevin listened carefully. "Verse one says, 'I am the true vine, and my Father is the husbandman.' One important job of a husbandman, or gardener, is to prune fruit trees."

To illustrate his message, the pastor told of helping his father prune the apple trees in his orchard. "Dead branches were the first to go. We cut them off and tossed them into a pile. Then Dad would take out the ones he had marked that hadn't borne fruit. Finally, he removed branches that crossed and rubbed against the good, fruit-producing branches. Let's talk of those troublemaking branches first. Do you know who I'm talking about?"

Kevin tried to recognize himself in each category of branches, and by the time all three unfruitful branches had been discussed and deemed unworthy, he decided it didn't matter where he fit. All three piles of branches ended up in the same bonfire while only the fruitful branches remained on the tree. His heart pounded when the organ began playing softly and the pastor asked any who wanted prayer to come forward. When no one stepped out by the end of the song, the congregation stood for prayer. Kevin breathed easier, and his heartbeat returned to normal.

"Wow!" Kevin drove away from the church. "I didn't get all that when I read that chapter last night."

Sarah turned to look at him. "You mean that's what you've been reading? Pastor Drake preached on the same scripture?"

"Yeah, quite a coincidence, huh?" Kevin shook his head. In his mind, he could still see the flames licking at the pile of unproductive branches. The pastor told a good story, one you could see in vivid detail.

"I guess so." Sarah turned toward the side window. "Where are we going? This isn't the way back to my house."

Kevin shot a grin her way, glad to be back in a normal conversation. "I thought we'd make up for last night. Lou Mitchell's should be open now."

Sarah stared at him for a moment and then started laughing.

"What?" His eyes twinkled even as he frowned. "You wouldn't be laughing at me, would you?"

"Of course." Sarah's laughter slowed to a chuckle. "You're going to Lou Mitchell's Restaurant because it's a landmark of Route 66."

"That isn't true." Kevin tried to look offended. "I'm going because I have a craving for Milk Duds. I've heard they give those away at the door."

Sarah held up her pointer finger and waved it back and forth. "No, no, no. Milk Duds are only for the ladies, which you, sir, are not."

He grinned. "I know you'll share."

She shrugged and looked out the side window before turning back with a sweet smile. "We'll see."

Love for Sarah filled every corner of Kevin's heart. What he'd felt as a boy was nothing to what he felt for her now. If only he could be sure of her love, or even that she no longer hated him. Every time he thought she'd let her guard down, something stopped her from getting too close, almost as if an invisible wall still separated them. He thought giving her the house would tear down that wall, but he didn't know yet. It was too soon to tell.

He parked, and they went inside the restaurant and found an empty booth. When their sandwiches came, Kevin hesitated only a moment before he reached across the table to take Sarah's hand. "Last night you asked me to pray before we ate. I think we should make this a habit."

Her smile wavered, but her nod was certain, so Kevin bowed his head and spoke in a low voice. "God, we ask that You bless our food. In Jesus' name we pray. Amen."

When he looked up, Sarah's smile was like a benediction to his prayer, but all she said was, "Thank you, Kevin."

He nodded and took a bite of his sandwich. "Remember, you are sharing those Milk Duds."

She patted her purse and lifted her eyebrows. "I'll try to remember. Of course, you still have donut holes for dessert."

He chuckled. "Yeah, right. What we haven't already eaten."

After they finished the sandwiches, she dug her Milk Duds out, and they polished them off while he drove to Sarah's house and stopped in her driveway. They walked to the front porch holding hands. Sarah unlocked the door and turned to him. "Would you like to come in?"

"No, not now, but I want you ready tomorrow right after work. What time do you get home, or should I pick you up at the hospital?"

Sarah's eyes widened. "Maybe you should tell me what you have in mind."

He put a hand on each of her shoulders and pulled her closer to him. "You, Sarah, are going with me tomorrow to shop for our son's graduation gift."

"Oh."

Kevin quickly kissed her very kissable-looking lips and grinned at her surprise. "Now, what time and where do I pick you up?"

"Let's not waste time. Be at the hospital's front entrance at three thirty. Do you have any ideas? Places we should shop?"

He shrugged. "Start with the mall, I guess."

"Okay. I'll try to think of gift ideas, and you do the same."

"Yes, ma'am." Kevin grinned. He tugged her closer and looked into her wide blue eyes. "May I kiss you?"

Her lashes lowered as if she were shy. "Why sir, I do believe this is the first time you've asked me that question."

Kevin crooked his finger under her chin and lifted until she looked him in the eyes. Then with studied slowness, he lowered his head until his lips covered hers in the sweetest kiss he'd had in a long time.

His breath came quick but so did hers, and there was satisfaction in that. For long moments their gazes interlocked, until finally she broke away. "If you aren't coming in. . ."

"No, I'd better get home. I'll be at the hospital. Three thirty, right?"

"Right." She stepped into the house, holding the edge of the door in front of her as she watched him.

He wanted another kiss, but he turned away and ran down the walk to his car before he took more than he should.

Monday afternoon Sarah left the hospital with the same question eating at her mind that had tormented her for the last twenty-four hours. *What am I doing?*

This was the third day in a row she would be spending time with Kevin. Her heart pounded in anticipation as if she were a teenager. He would break her heart just as he did before. Certain of that but finding no power to turn from him, she walked out the entrance and searched the area for the one man she longed to see.

She watched him hurry up the walk toward her and knew when he saw her by the smile that lit his face. She ran down the wide cement walk toward him.

"Sorry I'm late." He took her hand, and they walked back the way he'd come. "I intended to go to your office." He grinned. "Figured if the good doctor saw me, he'd back off."

Sarah gave him a reproachful look. "Doctor Jenson is a good man and a good friend."

Not to mention a problem she needed to do something about. His ring still sat on her coffee table. If only she could return it without hurting their friendship.

"Maybe so." Kevin looked away. "Sorry I mentioned him. Let's compare our ideas for Trey's gift."

"Fine. I hope your ideas are better than mine." Sarah counted off her list. "I thought of jewelry, sporting goods because he likes that sort of thing. Maybe tickets to another game. Clothing. I don't know."

Kevin gave a short laugh. "So at the mall we go to a clothing store, jewelry store, and athletic department. That narrows it down some. Let's see what we'll find."

An hour later they walked out of the mall empty-handed. Kevin held the car door for Sarah and then slid behind the wheel. "Nothing seems good enough for Trey."

She agreed. "I know. Any suggestions?"

"Yeah, one, but it'll cost you."

"How much?" Sarah searched his face. "What are you thinking?"

"He said he wanted a car."

She gasped. "Kevin, he was joking. His mom called him down on that, too. His parents would never let us buy him a car."

Kevin pulled his cell phone from his pocket. "How do you know if you don't ask?"

Sarah watched him push a couple of buttons and realized he had Trey's number programmed into his phone. He winked at her. She closed her mouth and waited. He could find out on his own.

"Tom? This is Kevin."

She heard the rumble of a male voice but couldn't understand the words.

"No, that's fine. Actually, you're the one I need to talk to." Kevin glanced at her. "Sarah and I are looking for a gift for Trey's graduation. We've come up empty at the mall and wondered if you'd object to us looking in a car dealership."

Again the rumbling and Kevin laughed. "I think we can afford it since we're going together on a gift anyway."

They talked for a few more minutes before Kevin told Tom good-bye and turned off his phone. He grinned at Sarah. "He says it has to be used."

"That's quite a gift, Kevin. Are you sure they won't resent us doing this? Maybe think we're trying to win Trey's affection from them?" Sarah wondered how she would feel in a reversed situation.

Kevin started his car. "It'll be fine. He didn't seem to mind at all. He just didn't want us spending more than we needed to. He says Trey's driving a real clunker now. Tom didn't say, but I know Trey would like a Mustang. Let's see if we can find a good used one."

They didn't find anything at the first place, but the second dealership had a midnight blue Mustang that Sarah thought was perfect—only two years old, and the asking price was reasonable.

"Are you sure this is the one?" Kevin folded his arms and eyed the car.

She nodded. "Can we take it for a test drive?"

The little car drove as smooth as she expected. Kevin let her drive a short distance, and she fell for the car even more. "Do you think they'll come down if we pay cash?"

Kevin grinned. "Exactly what I was thinking."

In the showroom, Sarah sat back and let Kevin haggle with the salesman and then the owner of the dealership. She held her breath until the owner shook his head. "I'm sorry, but I can only drop the price by a couple of thousand."

Her heart pounded as Kevin reluctantly agreed.

"All right. If you'll get those tires replaced, you've got a deal." He shook hands with both men and stood. "How soon will the papers be ready?"

"Is tomorrow afternoon soon enough?"

Kevin glanced at Sarah and she nodded. He turned back to the salesman. "That'll be fine. How about six o'clock? Will that work for you, Sarah?"

She nodded again. "Yes, that's fine."

Kevin put a deposit down on the car; they shook hands with the salesmen again and left. Sarah almost skipped to Kevin's car. "I'll withdraw some money from savings tomorrow for you. We can put the Mustang in my garage until Trey's graduation."

"Sounds good." Kevin grinned at her. "I can't wait to see Trey's face."

"I know." Sarah grabbed Kevin's hand and squeezed it between both of hers. "He's going to be so surprised."

She couldn't stop the laughter that bubbled. When Kevin's laughter joined hers, she felt more complete than she had in years.

twelve

On Tuesday evening, Kevin and Sarah drove to the car dealership to close the deal. When they walked out to the parking lot, he dangled two sets of keys in front of Sarah.

"I'm driving the Mustang to the graduation, so what's your choice tonight?" He held his keys closer to her with his dimples flashing. "My car?"

"Are you kidding?" She grabbed the other set of keys. "If this is my only chance, I'm driving the Mustang."

"Figures." His pout didn't sway her in the least. "Give a woman a choice, and she takes advantage of you."

"Ha, who's driving to Trey's hometown?" Sarah skipped ahead to the dark blue car and opened the driver's door. "That's a two-hour drive."

"Yeah." Kevin held the door for her while she sank into the car. "And it's this coming Saturday. We'll have to caravan down, so what are you driving? Mine or yours?"

"Mine." She didn't hesitate. "I'm used to my car. Have you eaten?"

Kevin grinned. "No, are you offering?"

Sarah's traitorous heart jumped at his nearness, the grin she loved so well, and the way he looked at her as if she were the only woman in the world. She tried to ignore the effect he had on her as she answered. "Sure, we'll be at my house anyway. I've got a couple of sandwich spreads in the fridge and a bag of chips. Sound nutritious enough?"

He patted his midsection. "Sounds great. I'll follow you."

He closed the door, gave her a quick wave, and strode to his car.

Sarah drove across town and pulled into her driveway with a sigh of relief. She already loved the little car, and she knew Trey would, too. She wanted it perfect for him, with no scratches or dents.

She waited while Kevin opened the garage door using her key, and then she drove inside and stepped out of the car. "It drives great. I'm really excited about this, Kevin."

He slipped his arm around her shoulders as they walked together around the car, looking and checking again for blemishes. At the back, Kevin nodded. "Yeah, we got a good deal, I think."

Sarah slipped from his arm and out of the garage. "I know we did. If you'll close the door, I'll bring my car back into the drive. I don't like leaving it on the street too long."

She swung around. "Oh, you have my keys."

"Tell you what." Kevin took her hand and led her toward the front door of her house. "I'll let you in, and then I'll move your car while you get supper started."

His words were commonplace, his actions no more than a friend. Still, a strange feeling of rightness settled over Sarah. Had she and Kevin become a couple again? Did buying a car together and fixing a meal at home mean anything? Maybe not to Kevin, but to Sarah, it meant everything.

❧

Wednesday morning Harold stopped to see Sarah while she was interviewing a woman for the business office. He left a message for her to meet him in the cafeteria at lunch.

She paid for her salad and crossed the dining room with slow steps. She hadn't seen him in several days and hadn't thought of him in just as long. She'd been busy. Buying a car took time. She lifted her chin and increased her pace.

"Hi, Sarah." Harold greeted her without his usual smile. "Sit down."

Sarah set her tray on the table and slid into the chair across from him. "I got your message. Is anything wrong?"

"I don't know." His forehead creased. "Maybe you can tell me. I haven't talked to you since Friday night. Where have you been?"

Sarah's eyes widened. "Why, right here, of course. What are you talking about? If you wanted to talk to me, all you had to do was stop by or call."

"I couldn't stop by, and I tried to call."

"Why not?"

Harold blinked. "Why not what?"

"Why couldn't you stop by? I've been at work every day this week. You found my office today." Sarah tried to keep her voice calm, in spite of Harold's unreasonable attitude.

He stared at her for several moments before saying, "I've been gone, Sarah. I got home only this morning, and I came straight to your office."

The seminar. Her face burned while her heart sank. How could she have forgotten? Kevin. He'd so filled her time and thoughts there'd been room for little else and certainly not Harold.

"I see you remember now." She cringed from the sarcasm in his voice. "I called your cell phone and your house phone several times Saturday night. I knew you were out with"—he paused as if the name was distasteful—"Kevin."

"I must have left my cell at home." She almost whispered the words.

"Sunday afternoon?"

She looked up. "I never take my phone into church."

"I said afternoon."

"Oh. I went out to eat right after church."

"Sunday night?"

She thought back and remembered curling up in bed with her Bible. She'd heard the phone ring downstairs, but let the answering machine pick up. She'd been too busy Monday to check her messages. Tuesday after work, she'd found two messages from Harold, but hadn't returned the calls. At the time, soaking in a bubble bath before Kevin arrived had seemed more important.

Now she focused on Harold. "I'm sorry, honest. I was reading my Bible Sunday night, then Monday and Tuesday I went gift shopping for Trey's graduation." Her eyes widened. "Oh, Harold, you'll never guess what we bought him. A car. A Mustang. It's only two years old and it's midnight blue. I know he'll love it."

Harold's eyebrows shot up and his mouth dropped open. "You bought a new car for. . .for. . ."

He couldn't seem to finish his sentence, so Sarah helped him. "Trey. For our son."

When he still stared at her, she said, "Okay, he isn't technically our son. I mean not legally, but in our hearts he always will be."

His eyes narrowed. "So you spent the last two nights with your high school boyfriend."

A short laugh escaped without mirth. "Hardly. Just a few hours shopping."

She stood, her salad practically untouched, and tried to keep annoyance from her voice. "I'm sorry you couldn't get through, Harold. It was one of those things. I've got to get back to work. As a father, you should understand how important Trey is to me. He always has been, but now we've met—" She hesitated. "I don't know. Maybe this is something only understood by those who experience it."

He stopped her with a hand on her arm. "I'm sorry, Sarah. I didn't mean to come down on you. I'm jealous. I admit it. Just the thought of you with that guy turns me inside out. I expected an answer by now. Why don't I come over tonight? We could watch a movie and popcorn. Talk about our future."

"I'm sorry, Harold." Sarah shook her head. "I have a meeting tonight. But you don't know our good news, do you?"

She sat back down and clasped his hands across the table. "Kevin found a house for us, and he gave it to us free and clear. It's a big, old Victorian in an older, but very nice neighborhood. There are seven bedrooms, a large kitchen, and a living room. It's perfect for the girls."

"Well, isn't that nice of him?"

"Yes, it truly is." Before she started gushing about Kevin's generosity, Sarah stood again. "I'm sorry you couldn't get hold of me, Harold. My intention was not to slight such a good friend, but with Trey's graduation and then the house for the girls, it's been a hectic week. Now I've really got to get back to work. I'll let you know more about the house later."

Halfway back to her office, Sarah realized Harold had been talking about the ring still sitting on her coffee table. How could she have forgotten Harold's ring? How could she have so completely forgotten him?

≈

Thursday evening Kevin took Sarah out to eat. On Friday evening, they fixed supper at his apartment and watched a movie then made plans to drive to Trey's graduation the following afternoon.

Sarah bought three rolls of wide red ribbon Saturday morning and cleaned her house from top to bottom. She warmed leftover casserole for lunch and then started a load of laundry.

She checked the time. Only one o'clock. She cleaned the refrigerator. The washer stopped, so she put clothes in the dryer and then ran upstairs to her bedroom. Kevin would arrive at three thirty. She pulled the bright blue sundress and matching yellow and blue jacket she planned to wear from the closet and laid them across her bed. She might as well take a shower and get ready while she had time.

Thirty minutes later, Sarah emerged from her bedroom, ready to go with an hour and a half to wait. She ran downstairs, grabbed up the phone, and punched in Kevin's number.

When he answered, she said, "Would we get there too early if we left now?"

His laughter filled her ear. "Sarah, you sound like a child who doesn't want to wait for Christmas."

"All right, so I'm a little eager."

"A little?" He chuckled. "You caught me pacing the floor."

"Are you ready?"

"Yeah, and chompin' at the bit."

"Why don't you come over here?" Sarah looked out the front window as if she would see Kevin driving down the street. "We could wait together."

"Good idea. I'll be right there."

Sarah hung up the phone and paced from one end of her house to the other until Kevin pulled into the driveway. She flung the door open and met him outside on the walk. "What took you so long?"

Kevin smiled. "You don't have much patience, do you?"

"Ha." She planted her hands on her hips and walked backward in front of him. "I've waited eighteen years for this day. If that isn't patience, I don't know what is."

His eyes held a message of love, but all he said was, "I understand. Let's get your stuff together and get started. Did you get the ribbon?"

Sarah twirled around and ran to the door. "Yes."

❧

Kevin stood just inside Sarah's door to wait while she gathered her purse, camera, cell phone, and the ribbon. She looked so feminine and beautiful in a blue and gold dress with her blond hair pulled back in a fancy braid. His gaze lingered on the neat hairdo that started on top of her head then looped around at the nape of her neck as if there were no end. Love for her filled his heart. Walking away from Sarah had been the biggest mistake of his life. Their past couldn't be changed, but they were together now, and that was all that mattered. If he asked her to marry him, what would she say? His heart pounded as if she'd already turned him down.

"Ready to go?" She stood before him, with a smile, and handed him a bottle of cold water. "Here you go. I took a couple from the fridge, so we don't have to stop on the way."

"Beautiful and smart, too." He grinned as a pink tinge sprang to her cheeks at his flattery. He glanced at his watch. "It's almost three, so we won't be more than an hour early."

"We could drive slow."

He laughed, took the bag of ribbons from her, slipped his arm around her shoulders, and opened the door. "Come on. Let's go."

Sarah led the way in her car. Kevin followed in the Mustang. He wanted to keep her in sight all the way, to know she was safe, but mostly to pretend she was his to protect and care for. When they finally reached the outskirts of Trey's hometown, Kevin slipped his cell phone from his pocket and called Sarah.

"What's wrong?"

He chuckled. "Is that the way you're supposed to answer a phone?"

"It is when my son's new car is at stake."

"The car's fine, but I'm hungry, and it's only five. We might as well grab a hamburger while we have time."

She groaned. "Time in abundance, you mean. We've got two hours. We should've waited at home. We can't eat for two hours."

At that moment, Kevin saw a sign that said CITY PARK with an arrow pointing to the left. "Maybe we can. I just got a craving for fried chicken and a picnic. Let's go to a deli and get the works, and then check out the park."

"I see a grocery store ahead. It looks big enough for a deli.

Follow me." Sarah's left blinker flashed while she waited for traffic to clear.

They passed a sprinkling of fast-food places, and Kevin recognized a couple more ahead. He preferred the choices in a grocery store to any of them. He and Sarah had always agreed on the important things in life. He smiled. Like buying a car for Trey. Today they were privileged to be included in Trey's life, in one of his greatest accomplishments by graduating from high school. Tonight he would pass from a boy to a man. Kevin was every bit as excited as Sarah to be allowed to watch, even from the sidelines.

❧

In the store, they bought crispy fried chicken, coleslaw, potato salad, baked beans, a pan of brownies, paper plates, plastic forks, napkins, and a quart of milk. When they left the store, Kevin put the bags in Sarah's car.

He took a deep breath before setting them on the floor. "Mmm. As good as this stuff smells, we don't want Trey thinking we ate in his car."

Sarah laughed. "Plus, we don't want you snitching any before we get to the park."

"Ha, and you aren't tempted?" He closed the back door and opened the front for her.

She slid in and gave him a sweet smile. "Even if I was, I couldn't reach anything. You put it behind me."

He grinned. "With good reason, ma'am. Follow me to the park."

Other than one young family playing on the swings, the park was deserted. Sarah chose a shelter with tables well away from the playground and began unloading their purchases on the table. Kevin sat down and watched her while they ate. "Do you miss small town life?"

She looked at him, her eyes wide. Finally she shrugged. "I don't know. I like the city, the convenience, my job, my house.

I visit Mom and Dad several times a year. That's enough for me, but—"

She looked around the rolling hills of the park. Wide cement walks meandered through an expanse of closely cropped thick green grass. Trees, some flowering, the others standing tall and green against the light blue sky, provided shade as well as beauty. The children in the playground shouted out their joy.

"But?" Kevin prompted her.

Her gaze settled on him and she smiled. "There's something special about small towns, isn't there? The pace is slower, the air is cleaner, there isn't as much noise." She laughed. "Everyone knows everyone else's business."

Kevin grinned. "That's true."

They talked about nothing and ate almost everything until a honeybee stopped to investigate the new aroma. Kevin swatted at the bee.

"Oh, don't hurt it." Sarah waved her hand over her plate when another bee made an appearance. "They pollinate the flowers."

"And fruit, but they also have stingers, and there's no pollen on my plate." He fanned two away. They were quickly replaced by another bee.

"Okay, that's it." Kevin swept their plates from the table and dumped them in the trash barrel in the corner of the shelter. "Maybe that will get rid of the attraction."

Sarah giggled. The bees were a nuisance, but she figured they were more interested in leftovers than in stinging. She cleared the table of trash.

Kevin watched her.

She smiled at him. "Isn't it time to go yet?"

He laughed and looked at his watch. "Yeah, it's after six. Let's see if we can find the football field."

They drove across town to the school. Sarah was eager to see Trey, but Kevin filled her thoughts. They'd spent over an hour in the park talking more than eating. Nothing of importance had been said. In fact, she didn't remember most of their conversation.

What she couldn't get out of her mind was Kevin's dark brown eyes crinkling at the corners, sparkling with amusement, or stealing her breath with their intensity. She loved watching his dimples deepen beside a smile that had always given her heart problems. In fact, she loved everything about Kevin.

All the past hurts had been healed. The hate she'd clutched so close for eighteen years fled before the love that now filled her heart. She no longer needed to hate. The love she'd hidden behind a facade of anger and resentment for much too long had been set free. She laughed with the sheer joy of loving Kevin and knowing he cared for her. He hadn't used words of love, but she saw his heart in his expressive eyes every time he looked at her. Why would he speak of love when she held herself from him?

She followed him into the school parking lot and stopped her car close to the exit. Kevin drove to the far edge and parked to one side. Sarah locked her car then ran past several parked cars to the Mustang.

He watched her come and lifted the bag of ribbons. "Think we can wrap this up pretty?"

"Of course." She took a roll of red ribbon from him and pulled the tape from the end. "All you have to do is crawl under the car with this, and then we'll tie a pretty bow on top."

"Ha, ha." Kevin took the roll from her and opened the front door. He positioned the end of the ribbon under the door and pressed the tape in place then closed the door, effectively securing the ribbon.

"Hey, smart man." Sarah ran around to the other side with another roll and did the same thing. "Now we have to tie a bow on top."

Kevin held the bag up. "You have another roll. Let's see if we can get it to stick to the back and front bumpers."

Sarah wasn't sure how long the tape would hold to the bumpers, but by the time they finished, they had Trey's Mustang tied in the wide red ribbon with a large bow on top. If no one bothered it during the ceremony and the wind didn't blow it off, they should be in good shape.

Sarah turned from the car to a rapidly filling parking lot. Almost everyone who walked past smiled or pointed at their gift. They were attracting a considerable amount of attention. "Kevin, we'd better get away from the car before Trey sees us."

"Yeah, I noticed." He took her hand, and they blended into the steady stream of parents, grandparents, siblings, and friends of Trey's classmates.

They found seats midway up on the bleachers. A large, wooden platform with steps on either end made an outdoor stage. The school band took their places to the side and began playing the processional, while the graduates marched past to fill the folding chairs waiting for them. Sarah strained to see and recognize Trey among all the blue and gold. She ignored the girls dressed in gold, but the blue caps and gowns made all the young men look the same.

"There he is." Kevin lifted his hand in a wave as so many others were doing.

Sarah wondered how the kids recognized their family in the closely crowded bleachers. She stood and waved in a wide arch.

Trey smiled at someone on the front row. Then he looked up and saw her, and his smile widened just as she snapped a picture. Sarah sat back down and clutched Kevin's arm. "He saw us."

Kevin chuckled. "How could he miss?"

Sarah ignored his teasing. They listened to the speeches and the special music. A girl sang a solo; then the entire class stood and sang their school song. Sarah laughed and squeezed Kevin's hand when Trey received three scholarships to college. Finally, under a darkening sky, the graduates walked across the stage to receive their diplomas.

During the recessional, Sarah watched the young men and women file out with wide smiles on their faces. Trey lifted his diploma high in a sign of triumph as he marched past. He sent a wide smile toward her and Kevin before joining his classmates, who had gathered on one end of the football field. With a cheer that rang loud and long, their caps sailed high into the night sky, lit by the football field floodlights. That was the signal Sarah had been waiting for. She wanted to get to Trey.

"I hope we haven't lost him." Sarah held to Kevin's hand as he led her down the bleachers.

"Not a chance. There's his parents." Kevin indicated the Millers talking to another couple as they made their way toward their son. "Let's catch up with them."

When the Millers welcomed them with open smiles and handshakes, Sarah realized she felt no competition with them for Trey's love. So many times when he was little, she had visualized Mrs. Miller holding her baby and resented the woman he would think of as his mother. Later, when he was older, she wished she could be the one to help him through life's problems. Even as recently as a few months ago when they first met, she'd fantasized him calling her Mom as some special bond between mother and son brought them together, as if all the years of separation had never occurred.

But there was no bond special enough to erase all the years of love and sacrifice from his adoptive family. She listened to his parents brag on their son and his accomplishments, and she knew. They were Trey's real family. While he'd inherited physical traits, personality, and temperament from her and Kevin, his mannerisms, lifestyle, beliefs, and memories came from his parents. She understood now what the Millers had known all along. Trey Miller was a product of all four adults who loved him so much. Trey was a very fortunate boy indeed. Or as her mother would say, Trey had been blessed mightily.

Sarah fell into step with Mavis, while Kevin walked behind with Tom. Trey ran to meet them from the confusion of his classmates calling out greetings and congratulations to others.

"Hey, are you coming to my party?" He threw out the invitation, taking them by surprise.

Sarah tried to convey with a quick glance at Kevin that she didn't want to stay. Trey would be with his friends and family tonight. They had no business imposing on his special time.

Kevin shook his head. "I wish we could, Trey, but it's getting pretty late, and we've got a long drive ahead. Before we go, though, we'd like to give you your gift. Would you all have time to walk us out to the parking lot? We didn't want to hold on to it during your graduation."

Sarah stifled a smile. They didn't want to hold it? She noticed the older Millers exchanged a smile.

"Sure," Trey said. "We need to get to the church for the party, anyway. It's actually for another guy, too. But, hey, you didn't have to get me anything. I'm just glad you both came."

"I'm glad, too." Kevin clapped a hand on Trey's shoulder, and they led the way to the parking lot. Sarah hurried to catch up and fell into step beside Trey with his parents following.

When they neared the Mustang, Sarah watched Trey. She knew he saw it, but he didn't say anything. Kevin led them to the driver's side. Trey's head turned as he looked the car over. The ribbon in back had come loose and flapped in the breeze like a red flag. Kevin and Sarah stopped, facing the Mustang. Trey swung with wide eyes toward Kevin first and then

Sarah. He turned to his smiling parents then looked back at Kevin. "Why'd you stop here?"

Before Kevin could answer, a group of kids walking by from several feet away called out, "Hey, Trey. Is that yours?"

"Is it?" Trey almost whispered.

"Yes." Sarah touched his arm.

"It's from Sarah and me." Kevin held out a set of keys. "Why don't you start it up? See if you like it."

"Oh, I like it." Trey blinked at the keys as if he didn't see them and turned to his folks. "Dad, Mom. It's a car. A Mustang."

"I can see that." His mother laughed. "Just what you've always wanted."

"Yeah." Trey seemed to be in a daze. Or maybe he didn't really like the car. Sarah held her breath and watched.

His dad pointed to the keys Kevin still held. "Try it out, son. See how well it runs."

"It's okay?" Trey looked at Kevin. "I mean, a car? I expected a book or, I don't know, maybe a shirt. But a Mustang?"

He took the keys and touched the door handle as if he still couldn't believe the car was his. Then, as if reality hit him all at once, he pulled the door open and let out a whoop of delight that pierced their ears and eased Sarah's concern. She laughed when he turned to his classmates who had formed a semicircle of curiosity and speculation around them. "Hey, the Mustang's mine."

In a lower voice, while his friends cheered and called out congratulations, he said, "We saw it sitting here when we walked past from the auditorium where we put our gowns on. I mean, you can't miss it with that bow on top. Everyone tried to figure out who the lucky guy was. Man, I never figured it'd be me."

He started to sit down and stopped, moving forward instead to take Sarah and Kevin into a group hug. Sarah soaked up the feel of his strong young arm around her, and she squeezed him tight. When he let go much too soon for her, she looked up through a mist of tears to see Kevin's eyes were also moist. He smiled at her, and she stepped into the circle of his arm as Trey moved back.

"Thank you." Trey shook his head. "I don't know what else to say, but just thank you doesn't seem enough."

"How about you promise to always drive within the law?" Kevin smiled to soften his words. "We want you to enjoy your time behind the wheel and never take foolish chances. That will be thanks enough."

"Now you sound like my dad." Trey laughed, and everyone ignored the double meaning of his words. "Don't worry. Mom and Dad have both drilled that into me already. I drive like a granny."

"Good, I'm glad to hear it. Grannies live to be old."

❧

Sarah handed her keys to Kevin and let him drive home. She relived the short time they'd spent with Trey and his reaction to the car. "He liked it, didn't he?"

Kevin grinned across the car at her. "He loved it. He's a good kid. He'll take care of it and appreciate what he has."

"Yeah." Would he have been such a good kid if they'd raised him? What about now? If they had another child, would they do as good a job as Mavis and Tom had?

Sarah straightened and glanced at Kevin. Warmth filled her cheeks. But Kevin wasn't looking at her, and thankfully, he couldn't read her mind.

She relaxed again and accepted the fact that she loved Kevin. She always had. The hate she'd fostered had been hurt and a cover for the pain of his rejection. But looking back from an adult viewpoint, she realized he'd done the only thing he could. His parents had threatened to turn away from him if he continued seeing her. He couldn't have married her without their permission, and her parents wouldn't have let her marry so young, either. They were all better off the way things had turned out. Trey and them, too.

They drove in companionable silence for several miles. Sarah closed her eyes and leaned her head back, trying to clear her mind of the new feelings of love that were so familiar yet even more intense now. Maybe if she ignored her feelings she wouldn't be hurt again, and she could keep Kevin's friendship.

She must have dozed off because when she opened her eyes, Kevin had already turned down her street.

"Hey, sleepyhead, did you enjoy the trip?" He grinned at her.

She laughed. "I'm sorry. Too much excitement, I guess."

"Worn out, huh?" The tenderness in his eyes brought a rush of love for him.

"Not now." She straightened, turning slightly toward him, and wished the evening would never end. "I've had my nap. Would you like to come in?"

He pulled into the driveway, expertly squeezing in beside his car. He opened the door and stepped out. "Come on. I'll walk you to your door."

By the time she had her purse in hand, he opened her door.

"Are you coming in?" she repeated, afraid to tell him the truth, that she didn't want him to leave.

He held her hand as they walked to the porch. "Would you be upset if I don't? I want to go to church with you in the morning, but tonight I think you're as tired as I am. Let's plan on spending the whole day together. We'll talk then."

He cupped his hand around the back of her neck and drew her closer as they stood in front of her door. "Right now, this is what I want."

Any remaining brick from the wall she'd built against him crumbled into fine dust and blew away with his kiss. Her heart soared, and love for Kevin filled every part of her mind and emotions. If he'd ask her to marry him, she'd say yes without hesitation. How she wished he would ask. They'd wasted far too many years.

❧

Sunday after church Kevin followed Sarah into her house and closed the door. She stopped with her hand on the banister leading upstairs and smiled at Kevin. "Make yourself at home while I change. I won't be long."

"Better not be." He grinned at her and headed toward the living room. Nervous energy carried him around the spacious room. He stopped in front of the fireplace and stared at a photo of Sarah's parents. Must be a recent one. There was one of her brother and Rachel Hawthorne. He remembered them, but he hadn't known they'd married. According to the picture, they had a couple of kids, too. He turned away from the obvious happiness on their faces, not wanting a reminder of his and Sarah's wasted years to spoil his plans for today and the future.

He sat on the couch and picked up a small red velvet box from the coffee table. A jeweler's box. He tossed it into the air a couple of times, catching it, then set it down. He stared at the box. Why would Sarah leave an old ring box on the coffee table in an otherwise immaculate room? He reached for it again and, with no expectations, opened it.

Kevin stared at the engagement ring in the box for a full ten seconds before he allowed his mind to accept what he saw. The white gold ring held a cluster of small diamonds set together in such a way to blend into one, creating the illusion of a huge solitaire with a small diamond on either side. This wasn't costume jewelry. No doubt Sarah's doctor friend knew exactly how much it cost.

Sarah's gasp from the doorway alerted Kevin to her presence. He stood with the open box still in his hand. His heart broke at the look of guilt on her face. He had his answer. He threw the box back on the table and walked toward her.

thirteen

Kevin stopped within three feet of Sarah. "I kissed you, Sarah. You kissed me back. I've spent the last two months being jerked through every emotional hoop you held while you accepted house calls from the doctor."

"No," Sarah cried out, but the twin pools of blue in her eyes didn't sway him.

"Yes." He kept his voice quiet, emotionless, while a hammer shattered his heart with repeated blows of wrenching pain. He had to walk past her without touching. He had to leave before he broke down and begged her to let him stay. "I loved you once, Sarah. I shed more tears over losing you back then than I did all together the first years of my life. I haven't cried since, and I won't cry now. Fools who repeat their mistakes—"

He gave a snort of derision. "Let's just say, I won't be a fool a third time."

He ignored the tears running down Sarah's face and stepped past her, brushing so close, her warmth reached out to him.

"Good-bye, Sarah." Five long strides took him outside. He let the door close between them.

Kevin started his car and backed out of Sarah's driveway. At the stop sign he waited for another car to turn in front of him. The driver was beside him before his mind focused enough to recognize Harold Jenson. Sarah's doctor making another house call. But of course.

He almost felt sorry for the doctor. Sarah had played both of them for fools. Last night she'd kissed him as if she meant it while the doctor's ring waited on her coffee table. No doubt she enjoyed stringing two men along, playing some sadistic female game. She was a good actress. He'd give her that. She'd learned more playing Sadie the clown than how to help children relax and have fun. Obviously the light of love he'd seen in her eyes had been as fake as Sadie's red nose. Maybe she truly loved her doctor. Maybe not. He didn't care anymore. Doctor Jenson would have to figure out truth from fiction now.

⋈

The click of the door closing behind Kevin broke Sarah's disbelief. She ran after him, jerking the door open to see his car door close, sealing him away from her. On the porch, she clutched the railing and watched him leave. He drove away without a backward glance. He hadn't given her a chance to explain.

She'd lost him. Sobs shook her shoulders, and tears streamed from her eyes as she went back inside and sat on the sofa where he had been only moments before. She held the offending ring box in her hand and fell over against the sofa releasing a flood of tears against a pain so intense she felt as if she might die. After a few moments, the deep pain lost its edge, and the sobs stopped shaking her body. She'd survived the first time he walked away and she would again. Still, tears seeped from her eyes, and her heart ached as if a giant hand held it in an iron grip. This time she couldn't fall back on hate to ease the pain, because she didn't hate Kevin. She loved him, and she always would.

A quick knock sounded at her door before it opened and Harold stepped in. "Sarah, where are you?"

She sniffled and swiped a sleeve across her eyes.

He appeared at the door, took in her disheveled appearance, and crossed the room to sit beside her and hold her wrist in his fingers. "What did he do to you? Where are you hurt?"

She pulled away from him. "I'm fine."

"You're not fine. What happened here?" Harold touched her forehead then grasped her shoulders and slid his hands down her arms, looking from one to the other.

She jumped up and stepped out of his reach. "Will you stop examining me? I'm not hurt physically. I just—"

Lost the man I love.

"I got my feelings hurt. That's all."

"Do you want to talk about it?"

"No."

"Why don't we go get something to eat?" Harold stood and reached for her hand.

She pulled away before he could touch her. "I'm not hungry. I'd like to spend some time alone. I have things I need to do here."

The jeweler's box lay on the floor where it had fallen. She bent to pick it up and handed it to Harold. "I shouldn't keep this any longer."

He set it on the coffee table. "You're upset right now. Wait until tomorrow and you'll feel better. Am I still taking you to the open house Thursday for Marilee's Home?"

She hugged her arms, trying to bring warmth and feeling back into her body while she forced a smile for Harold's benefit. "Of course, I can't imagine anyone I'd rather go with."

That brought a smile to his face and guilt to her heart. She didn't want to encourage him. She didn't want to hurt him, because she knew how that felt. She moved toward the door, hoping he would take the hint.

He soon left with promises to return Thursday evening and to check on her tomorrow at work. She watched him drive away and breathed a sigh of relief. Until she turned and saw the ring box on the table.

❧

At Marilee's Home, Sarah stood in the parlor between Darlene and Harold, watching the girls escort other board members and benefactors through their new home. Their eyes sparkled above wide smiles as they explained how the house had come to be theirs. Seven girls. Already they had an addition, and thanks to Kevin, they had room for more. They'd all worked hard selecting used furniture and arranging each room. There'd been little repair or finishing work required on the house itself, so most of their efforts had gone to cleaning and furnishing. Kevin couldn't have given her a better gift.

As if her thoughts brought him to life, the door opened, and he stepped into the front hall. From her position, she watched him speak to the girl who'd let him in. He looked past her to small groups of two or three, then moved on as if searching for someone. He stopped and stared without expression as his eyes met Sarah's. She broke the contact when Darlene spoke to and left with someone else. When she glanced back he was escorting a young woman into the parlor.

"Are you all right?" Harold's low voice reminded her to breathe, although she hadn't known she'd stopped.

"Of course." Sarah spread her lips into what she hoped would pass for a smile.

The woman with Kevin was beautiful. Her dark hair, cut to touch her shoulders, moved as strands of silk with each toss of her head. She smiled easily, her dark eyes laughing and admiring Kevin in a familiar way that burned a hole through Sarah's heart. Kevin's possessive touch on the woman's arm, as they moved across the room, hurt more than Sarah could have imagined.

"Good evening, Dr. Jenson. Sarah." Kevin and his date stood in front of them. "The place looks good."

"Thank you. We've all worked hard the last couple of weeks." Sarah smiled at Harold. "Even Dr. Jenson got in on some heavy moving one night."

"How nice." Kevin let his gaze slide past Harold to Sarah

while he spoke to the woman at his side. "Valerie, this is Sarah Maddox and Dr. Jenson. Sarah is chairman of the board for Marilee's Home. She's actively involved with the girls and the running of this outreach. Sarah, I'd like you to meet Valerie Parker. She's a top-notch accountant and a good friend."

He gave the young woman a teasing smile. "She's also my boss's daughter."

Valerie laughed, took his arm, and leaned her head against his shoulder in a quick hug before straightening. "Kevin's a dear. He's always coming to my rescue. I don't know what I'd do without him."

He just smiled at her without comment. Sarah's stomach churned as she murmured the requested niceties to a woman she'd rather throw out the door.

"There's a table in the kitchen set up with punch, cookies, a cheese ball, crackers, just about anything you might want." Harold motioned toward the door leading that way. "Help yourself, we're informal and too lazy to serve."

Sarah appreciated his attempt at humor, but she didn't feel like laughing. Valerie did, though, and she pulled Kevin toward the kitchen.

"I want to see this old house. It's beautiful, Kevin. However did they find such a wonderful place?" Valerie's voice drifted back as Kevin followed her out of the room.

So he hadn't told her everything. Had he told her about Trey? And her? Somehow the idea Valerie didn't know Kevin's dearest secrets brought balm to Sarah's hurting heart.

She turned her attention to welcoming more potential donors as others came in, and the evening moved on until she realized she hadn't thanked Kevin publicly for the house. When she couldn't find him, she assumed he and his girlfriend had already gone. It was just as well. She didn't know if she could hold a smile much longer, anyway.

By the time the house cleared of visitors, Sarah welcomed

Harold's suggestion to leave. He remained silent on the drive home and walked her from the car without touching her. She unlocked her front door and turned to thank him for going with her, but he spoke first.

"May I come in? I promise I won't stay long."

Sarah nodded, wishing she could say no. All she wanted at the moment was to curl up in bed with her Bible and seek comfort for a broken heart.

She led the way into the living room and sank to the sofa. Harold stood.

"Do you want something to drink?" She looked up at him.

He shook his head. "No, I'm fine."

After a moment, he moved to sit beside her. "I've been patient, Sarah. You've had my ring almost three weeks. Each time I mention it, you offer to give it back. I had hoped with time. . .I guess I knew all along what your answer would be."

Sarah hadn't expected the pang of anxiety she felt with Harold's words. She counted him a friend, and she didn't want to lose him, but she didn't love him. Marrying him wouldn't fill the emptiness Kevin had left. She'd lost the only man she would ever love, not once but twice. Harold needed to find another mother for Katie. She wouldn't stand in his way.

Sarah picked up the ring box and handed it to Harold. "I'm sorry, but I'm not the wife you're looking for."

His fingers closed around the box, and his eyes met hers. "Maybe I'm not the husband you're looking for."

Tears sprang to her eyes, and she swiped at them. "No, I'll never marry."

"You're in love with him, aren't you?"

Sarah shook her head. Her hands twisted together in her lap. "He walked away from me twice."

A sob tore from her. Harold's arm slipped around her shoulders pulling her into a comforting embrace. "Oh Harold, how can I live without him now?"

"You could still marry me." He patted her back as if she were Katie.

She pulled away and stood. A mirthless laugh tore from her throat. "No, that would be wrong for both of us. I know that now. I didn't mean to string you along. I was afraid of losing your friendship."

He stood watching her, searching her eyes. "Are you sure you know what you're doing? Would marriage to me be so bad? Some of the best marriages have been based on friendship."

She shook her head. "I can't. You deserve better than that."

She grabbed a tissue from the table and walked to the front door with him following. She stepped out on the porch with him. "Good night, Harold. Please find someone who truly loves you and who you love with all your heart. I'm sorry it couldn't be me."

His smile didn't reach his eyes. "I had hoped. But I guess not. Will you send me off with one last hug? Groucho wants to stay friends with Sadie."

Sarah stepped into his embrace and felt nothing except warmth. Why couldn't she love Harold? A slow-moving car caught her attention and, still in Harold's arms, she watched it drive by. Was that Kevin? Sarah jerked back.

"I'm sorry—" Harold started to apologize.

"No, it's my fault." She stared down the street but saw only red taillights. "I've got to go in, Harold. Please don't settle for second best. God has someone for you. I know He does."

After Harold drove away, Sarah locked her door and headed upstairs. Had Kevin driven past her house, or was she seeing things? If only she could get Kevin Nichols out of her life and out of her heart for good.

fourteen

So much for talking to Sarah. Kevin drove away with a heavy heart, the image of her wrapped in the doctor's arms a clear picture in his mind. He'd lost her. Maybe if he'd found her sooner, before Jenson stole her heart, he might've had a chance.

At his apartment, he went to the kitchen and started coffee. While it percolated, he pulled his tie off and hung it in his bedroom. Back in the living room he sank into his recliner and lifted his Bible from the lamp table. Maybe while he waited for his coffee, he could erase Sarah from his mind.

By habit, he turned to the Gospel of John and began to read. After several minutes, he set his Bible aside and went to the kitchen, returning with a cup of coffee and a package of cookies. Again he picked up his Bible, letting it fall open to John 15. He skimmed over the first verses that he had almost memorized and read to the end of the chapter then returned to verse seven. "If ye abide in me, and my words abide in you, ye shall ask what ye will, and it shall be done unto you."

He closed the Bible and set it aside. How he wished he could believe that. If simply asking would bring Sarah to him, he would at least try. He finished his coffee, took the cookies back to the kitchen, and went to bed.

Kevin woke the next morning with the sheets twisted around his legs. He nicked his chin when he shaved, and he dripped milk from his cereal on his shirt. Could the day get any worse?

Mr. Parker stopped him before he reached his office. "Nichols, when you get a minute, come see me."

"Sure." Kevin nodded toward his office door. "Let me get settled, and I'll be right there."

His boss waved his hand as if brushing him aside. "No hurry. Just whenever is fine."

"Okay."

Kevin entered his office. He left the door open. "Good morning, Valerie. What are you up to now?"

She leaned back in his chair with her feet, crossed at the ankle, resting on his desk. He skimmed past the fair amount of smooth leg her dress didn't cover and met her gaze. She frequently dressed in vibrant colors. Today's choice of red set off her olive skin tones and dark hair to perfection. A welcoming smile and sparkling brown eyes completed the picture. "I've been waiting for you."

"I see." He leaned against the desk. "Is there a reason?"

Her feet hit the floor and she stood, coming around to stand beside him. "Of course, Kevin. I always have a reason for what I do."

He crossed his arms and faced her. "So that means you want something from me."

Her lower lip stuck out in a pretty pout. "You're being mean when I only want to invite you to church."

"Okay." Why not? He wouldn't be going with Sarah anymore.

"Okay, what?" Her pout gave way to puzzlement. "Okay to invite you, or okay you'll go with me?"

He let out an exaggerated sigh. "Where and when?"

The squeal took him by surprise but gave warning before she launched herself into his arms. He chuckled. "Valerie, is this the way to behave in a public place of business?"

He didn't expect her quick kiss on his lips, but she pulled back just as quick and twirled around, her skirt billowing out like a little girl's. He laughed with her, glad for the distraction from his self-pity. He circled his desk and sat down. "Why don't you run along now? I need to check on some things before I talk to your father."

She smiled and grabbed a pen and paper from his desk, then wrote something before handing it to him. "This is the church's address and the time. Don't you dare be late. I'll wait for you in front."

He glanced at the address and nodded. "I'll be there."

She swirled away and stopped a moment by the door. "We always go out to eat after church. See ya."

Twenty minutes later, Kevin knocked at John Parker's office before entering. His boss greeted him with a smile and a firm handshake. "Sit down. I won't take but a minute of your time. How are things going?"

"Fine." Kevin wasn't sure what else to say. His personal life had died a premature death, but Mr. Parker wouldn't be interested.

"Good." They talked shop for a while, until Mr. Parker leaned forward. "I've been watching you, Kevin. You take the initiative and get things done. I don't worry when you're out in the field, because I know we'll have a satisfied client when you come home. I like that. Valerie has nothing but good to say about you. I appreciate you taking her to the open house for that girls' home last night. Sorry the wife and I couldn't make it. She filled us in, though. From what she said, they got a nice place. My little girl may be a bit dingy sometimes, but she's got a good head on her shoulders. She knows quality when she sees it, and I'm not talking about the house. I mean her escort."

"Thank you, sir. I appreciate that." Did the man know his daughter was pushing past professional limits? The kiss she'd given him was about as chaste as any he'd ever experienced, but he didn't think Valerie intended to stop there. What would her father think then?

"So can we expect to see you Sunday?"

He'd obviously missed part of the conversation, but he caught the gist of it. He nodded. "Yes, I told Valerie I'd come."

"Good." Mr. Parker rose, signaling their time had ended. He extended his hand, which Kevin took for a quick shake. "Plan to eat with us at the club after."

"Thanks, I will."

Kevin went back to work, wondering at the turn his life seemed to be taking.

❧

Two days later, he entered church with a beautiful woman on his arm, but she wasn't Sarah, and the church wasn't Sarah's. He sat through the sermon, remembering the vivid word pictures Sarah's pastor used to bring God's Word to life. He looked down at his open Bible while the minister's voice droned on. He turned to the now familiar Gospel of John and let the thoughts of the fourteenth chapter lift him to a higher plane. How he would love the assurance of a place in heaven. Jesus told His disciples He would go away and prepare a place for them. A place to belong sounded pretty good to Kevin. At the moment he wasn't sure where he belonged.

Not with Sarah obviously. She'd told him to get lost when they were kids. She said she never wanted to see him again. Did she still feel that way? If so, she'd put on a good act, but for what purpose? Why had she led him on only to dump him for another man? To hurt him? His shoulders slumped with the heavy weight of his heart as he stood with the Parkers for the closing prayer.

The country club's dining room buzzed with activity, and Valerie kept a firm hold on Kevin's arm. She bestowed a sweet smile on him when he held her chair and sat at her side. Her parents sat across from them. While they ate, the hum of conversations and soft music over the speakers created background for a perfect meal of baked veal, fluffy mashed potatoes, and asparagus.

Mr. Parker mentioned his business with pride. "I started out as a CPA working for someone else. Decided I wanted my own business. The wife and I were newlyweds then, and I took a gamble. Everyone said I'd lose my shirt, but instead I latched on to a whole new wardrobe." He laughed at his joke.

Kevin smiled with him. "You've done very well for yourself. That's something to be proud of."

His boss nodded. "True, but I'm getting older now and don't figure I have the energy of a young man." He jabbed his fork toward Kevin. "It takes a lot of stamina to build and grow. That's for young men."

"Daddy, why don't you and Kevin continue this conversation at the office?" Valerie scooted her chair back. "I want to show Kevin around the grounds."

Kevin stood to help her with her chair. She smiled at him. "I don't mean to rush you, but Daddy can go on and on when he gets started."

Before Kevin could respond, Mr. Parker waved them away. "No, that's fine. You two take a walk. Mom and I may do the same a little later. I'll see you in the morning, Kevin. Stop by the office sometime during the day. I need to discuss something with you."

Kevin nodded. "All right. I'll see you tomorrow. If you don't mind, I'll see Valerie home after our walk."

Mr. and Mrs. Parker both smiled and nodded. "Take your time. Show him the pool, Val. Maybe he likes tennis or golf."

"Tennis might be fun. Too bad we aren't dressed to play." Just hearing the word *golf* brought back memories of Sarah at the miniature golf course. Memories that he shoved to the back of his mind now so he could continue to smile and appear interested in the walk Valerie wanted.

"We'll come back later when we are." Valerie smiled up at him, and he had to think for a moment what she meant.

"Oh yes, to play tennis. Do you have rackets, or should I stock up on a couple along with some balls?" He led her away from the table toward the door.

Her laughter sounded pure and real. "Daddy's been a member of the club all my life, so we have plenty of equipment. Don't waste your money. I love to play. Why don't we bring a change of clothes next Sunday, and we'll bat balls around for a while? No pressure. Just see how we do."

"No showing me up, huh?" He smiled at her. "Okay, I'm game if you promise to go easy on me."

"I do." Her dark eyes twinkled with an emotion he didn't want to decipher.

❧

Late Monday afternoon Kevin tapped on Mr. Parker's door. He'd been busy all day and had only a few minutes ago remembered his promise to stop by the boss's office. Valerie must've been busy, too. He'd seen her once and scarcely had time to return her smile before she hurried off.

"Come on in." Mr. Parker's gruff voice called out.

Kevin stepped inside.

"I've been expecting you." His boss motioned to the chair facing his desk. "Have a seat. I want to know what you thought of church. Our minister knows the Bible inside out, doesn't he?"

Kevin nodded. "Yes, he seems quite knowledgeable."

He couldn't argue with that. The man seemed to have an extensive knowledge of the history of Egypt and ancient Rome including the customs of the time. So what if he hadn't felt as if anything in the sermon applied to his life? A man would have to be egotistical to think every sermon he heard was preached for him alone. Maybe next week's sermon would be different.

"So are you planning to attend this coming Sunday?" Mr. Parker watched him as if his answer mattered.

"I promised Valerie I would."

A wide smile broke over the other man's face. "Great. We'll count on it then. That brings us to the reason for this meeting."

Until that point, Kevin hadn't thought much about his summons. Over the years he'd worked for Parker, he'd sat before him many times discussing one problem after another. Instinctively he knew this time was different. Not only from the gleam in his eyes but also by bringing church into the equation, Parker had more than business on his mind. As he talked, Kevin's suspicion grew.

"Parker Enterprises has grown beyond the scope of my original vision. I first expected a small office of accountants servicing the Windy City. We've gone beyond that, as your trips into Michigan and Indiana prove. We're right up there with commercial real estate, and our financial services are some of the best. There's still room for growth, but we've done well for ourselves."

He shifted in his chair. "I've had my eye on you, Kevin, since you joined our firm. You're a bright, energetic young man. Valerie thinks highly of you. I'd be proud to welcome you into the family, and I want you to know a partnership is yours if that happens. . . ."

Kevin heard the rumble of Mr. Parker's words after that, but he didn't try to listen. He'd heard all he needed to. Had Valerie put her dad up to this? She was spoiled enough to get away with such an underhanded trick, but why would she? She had her choice of men. She'd turned down two marriage offers he knew of. Why him? And why not? Sarah didn't want him. He wasn't getting any younger, and he'd like to have a family of his own someday. He liked Valerie and enjoyed her company. What more could a guy expect? Maybe he'd go along with her game and see where it took him. He didn't have to make a commitment right now.

❧

Sarah spoke into her phone at work. "Darlene, hello."

She winced, knowing she'd neglected Marilee's Home since the night of the open house. The night Kevin paraded his girlfriend in front of her. No, that wasn't fair. He probably thought she was engaged to Harold. He had every right to be with whomever he wanted. He could marry her for all she cared. Tears welled in her eyes, and she brushed them away with more force than necessary.

"How have you been?" Darlene's compassionate voice came over the phone, and Sarah straightened, bringing her thoughts back to her friend.

"Busy. You know how it is. Seems like there's always something to do." She picked up a pen and began doodling on a pad of paper.

"Oh, that's the truth, but what's it been? Two, three weeks?

The girls have been asking about you. They want to show you what they've done to their rooms." Darlene laughed. "It's amazing how each room reflects the personality of the girl. I think this house is more home to these girls than the one we wanted to keep. How wrong a person can be."

"Yes, that's true." She should have fought to keep Kevin, but she let him go twice. Now it was too late. It had been three weeks ago tonight since she saw him, but he'd stayed on her mind every second of that time. Twice she'd started to call him to explain, then couldn't. Not with that dark-haired woman's beautiful face standing between them. She'd been so wrong, and she lost him. He'd found someone else.

"So when do you think you'll have time for us?" Darlene asked.

"How would tomorrow night work?" She really did want to see the girls.

"Fine. Plan to stay for dinner. What's your favorite?"

Sarah stared in horror at her subconscious doodling. From every angle, Kevin Nichols's name in hearts taunted her. She threw the pen across her office to land in the soft carpeting. "My favorite? Have you had hamburgers and homemade fries lately?"

"Nope, but we can tomorrow." Sarah heard paper rustling. "I'll make a note for Grace. The girls will love it."

After Darlene hung up, Sarah retrieved her pen and tore the paper with Kevin's name to shreds before throwing it away. Forcing her mind back to work, she shut everything else out.

Sarah drove to the girls' home after work Friday. She was happy for the girls, and visiting them was no chore. They welcomed her with open arms and led her from one bedroom to another.

Cindy, her blond ponytail bouncing, pulled Sarah into her room. "What do you think? Pretty, huh?"

One of the other girls snickered. Sarah blinked at the intense pink glow dominating the room. Even the white walls took on a pink cast from the hot pink curtains hanging on the west window. The single bedspread matched the curtains, adding to the color.

"Oh my," Sarah said. "You won't get tired of this, will you?"

Cindy stuck out her chin. "Nope. I love pink."

"We were glad she got her own bedroom." One of the girls filling the doorway spoke up. She added in a loud whisper, "No one else could stand this much pink."

Another said, "Good thing she's having a girl. This room would ruin a poor little baby boy."

Sarah laughed before the teasing got out of hand. "Actually, the room is lovely, Cindy. I think the sun coming through the window is intensifying the color. Your room is neat and clean and I know that's your job, so don't let anyone sway you from your choices. You're doing great."

She looked at the other girls. "You all are. I'm glad to see you settling in here and making a home during what I know is a difficult time."

"You had a baby when you were in high school, right?" Cindy asked.

Sarah nodded. "Yes, I gave my son up for adoption to a wonderful couple."

"How do you know they were wonderful?" one of the girls asked. "Did you know them?"

"No, but I met them and their son a few months ago."

"Their son?" Cindy looked skeptical. "You mean your son?"

Sarah smiled. "He was my son until they came to the hospital and took him. He's their son now. I've spent some time recently with all three of them, and as much as I'll always love him and consider him my baby, he's made a place with his parents. I can see how close they are. How much he loves them and how much they love him. I'm a special friend now, and that's the way it should be."

"Wow!" Cindy shook her head. "I don't know. My mom wants me to give my baby away. She even had a social worker come and talk to me. She never said anything about me seeing her later on. I figured that was it. Once you gave your baby away, you never saw her again or knew anything about her."

"The people could be mean to her, and you'd never know." Some of the girls murmured among themselves.

"That's true." Sarah moved toward the door. "Why don't we go downstairs and talk where it isn't quite so pink?"

The girls' laughter eased the tension. She led the way. "I don't know a lot about adoption. All I do know is my own experience, but you can certainly ask your social worker about open adoption. That's where you have a say in choosing parents for your child. See if you have the option of meeting the adoptive parents before you make your final decision."

They settled in the parlor with Sarah on the sofa and two girls on either side of her. For a moment, she sat quiet, as the memory of her last time in the room rushed into her head and slammed against her heart. As if looking at a silent movie, she saw Kevin with his hand against Vickie's or Valerie's or whoever's back.

"How do you choose?" The girl's question intruded, and Sarah blinked to clear her mind of the memory she needed to forget.

"Um, home studies are done on prospective families and their homes. You should be allowed to look through the ones the social worker has picked. They get so many for each baby, you can't go through them all. They said there were fifty applicants for Trey. There would have been many more, but only people in a certain area were allowed to apply."

As the girls asked questions, Sarah tried to answer from her limited knowledge. She was glad when Darlene came in and told them the hamburgers were ready.

"It's so pretty out, we thought you would like to eat on the patio in back." Darlene laughed at the enthusiastic response as the girls stood and headed toward the kitchen.

Sarah was glad to leave the parlor, where Kevin's memory lingered like a foul odor. But when she walked into the kitchen, he again intruded as she remembered that night he'd surprised her with the house. They'd inspected the kitchen and every room. Hand in hand, they'd walked through the large Victorian. Her eyes burned, and she welcomed the evening breeze keeping them dry as she forced herself to eat and enjoy her time with Darlene and the girls. As the sun sank in the west, she left the warmth of their friendship and went home alone.

After a quick shower, Sarah curled up on her bed with her Bible and called Trey. When he came to the phone, he said, "Sarah, hi. Is everything all right there?"

She glanced at the clock and saw it was almost ten o'clock. "Yes, of course. I'm sorry. I just now noticed the time. I won't keep you." She gave a short laugh. "Mostly, I guess I just wanted to hear your voice. Make sure you're all right. I didn't think. It's Friday night, and you might not have been home."

"Speaking of that. . ." Trey sounded distracted. "Why don't I give you my cell phone number. Then it doesn't matter if I'm home or not. I don't know why I didn't do this before now."

"I don't want to bother you, Trey. I mean, what if I call when you're out with your friends? You wouldn't want that."

He chuckled. "I doubt you could interrupt anything important. You don't call often, so when you do, I want to be sure to answer. Here's my number."

Sarah grabbed a pen and paper from her nightstand and wrote down the numbers. "Okay, I got it."

"I want yours, too." He listened for her number and then said, "I text a lot, so that's good, too."

"Great, I'm a whiz at texting." Sarah laughed with him. She didn't know what to say next. Then she noticed the Bible she held in her arms as if it were Trey. "I've been reading my Bible. I'm in Ephesians now. I guess I'm skipping around."

"That's cool. I do that a lot, too." He hesitated before saying, "I think God's been talking to me lately. I mean, I'm going to college this fall, but maybe after that I'll go to seminary."

Sarah sucked in an extra dose of air. "You mean. . . ?"

He laughed. "Yeah, I mean preaching. As a pastor. I'm not rushing into anything. But when God calls, we need to answer."

"Yes, that's true." For some reason tears welled in Sarah's eyes, and she couldn't stop them from rolling down her cheeks. Thankfully Trey couldn't see her. "I'm so proud of you, Trey."

They talked for a few minutes more and then hung up. She lay back on her bed and stared at the ceiling while silent tears ran over her temples, wetting her hair. An unexplained longing for her mother filled her heart. Talking to Trey brought Kevin close yet left her feeling empty and alone. Mom's home-cooked meals and chocolate chip cookies would go a long way toward filling the void in her life. And Dad, too. She missed his hearty laughter and warm hugs. Amanda's family always held a Fourth of July cookout in their backyard. Would Amanda come this year?

With more enthusiasm than she'd approached anything in weeks, Sarah sat up and reached for her cell phone. California time was two hours earlier, but Amanda should be home now.

"Hello?"

"Hi, Amanda?" Her voice sounded as if she were just across town. "You sound so good."

Amanda laughed. "I am good. In fact, I feel like celebrating. Classes are over for the summer, and I have only one more semester to go. If you hop a plane you should be here in what? Two hours? By morning?"

Sarah's laughter felt good. "Oh, I wish I could. I'm so proud of you. It's been a long, hard road, hasn't it?"

"Yes, but I'm getting there." After they talked a bit, Amanda said, "God's been so real in my life lately. I plan to be home over the Fourth, Sarah, and I want you there. I talked to Tessa, too. She's coming with her husband and kids. I want to see both of you."

"I'll be there on the Fourth." No question in her mind now. She was going home.

&

After church Sunday, Kevin again shared dinner with his boss's family at the country club. Afterward, he and Valerie changed into casual clothing so they could play tennis. They met at the courts, and he took the racket she handed him.

"I haven't played since college. You may have to help me out." He grinned at her. "Or maybe we could call it a draw since all the courts are taken."

She laughed. "Not a chance. We're playing doubles. Follow me."

Her white shorts and sleeveless white shirt set off the golden glow of her skin and contrasted to her dark hair. At least she wouldn't be hard to look at across the table every morning. He caught up with her, and they walked together to the far court where another couple batted a ball across the net. They didn't appear to be playing a game and stopped at Kevin and Valerie's approach.

"Hey, you made it." The woman ran to Valerie for a quick hug. Her partner strolled across the court to shake Kevin's hand.

"Dave Walker." He introduced himself.

"Kevin Nichols." Kevin looked at the man, who appeared only a few years older. "I've heard your name. You're in real estate, aren't you?"

"That's right." Dave grinned. "You should know. I can't believe how many times you've snatched a good deal out from under my hand. You've got the instinct to know when to hold and when to let go. That's something you can't learn, my friend. It's a God-given talent."

Kevin saw sincerity in the other man's eyes. "Interesting way to put it. I've never thought much about what I do other than it's a gamble. Sometimes it pays off. Occasionally it doesn't."

"Feast or famine, huh?"

Kevin laughed. "That pretty much sums it up."

Dave lowered his voice and glanced toward the women, who had walked away talking. "If you ever get tired of operating on your own, come see me. I'm in construction as well as real estate, and I need a salesman." He pulled a business card from his pocket and handed it to Kevin. "If you can do what I think you can, I've got a place for you at a good salary plus commission."

Kevin took the card and stuck it in his pocket. The salary Dave mentioned was more than what he made at Parker's but less than a partnership would be.

He shook Dave's hand again. "Thanks. I'll think about it."

"Hey, you guys." Valerie waved her racket over her head. "We came to play tennis. Girls against guys. Think you can handle it?"

"Oh, that sounds like a challenge." Dave slapped Kevin on the shoulder. "Come on, buddy. Let's show them what they're up against."

"You bet." Kevin fell into step with Dave, who pointed his racket toward the girls.

"By the way, the pretty blond with Valerie is my wife, Suzy Walker." He called out, "Suzy, this is Kevin Nichols."

"Yes, I know." She smiled at Kevin. "Valerie's already told me about him. I'm glad to meet you, Kevin."

"Glad to meet you, too, Suzy." Kevin grinned at her as he walked past to take his place across the court from the women.

"Ooh, I love your fiancé's dimples." Suzy's soft comment, carried by a gentle breeze, had surely been meant for Valerie's ears alone.

Kevin bristled at Valerie's assumptions but chose to ignore the misunderstanding. The challenge had been issued. He just hadn't decided how to respond. Next week he'd be in Indiana, and after that he would spend the Fourth of July weekend with Trey. Maybe he'd be able to sort his feelings out then. Valerie deserved no less than an honest answer to the question he hadn't asked, but she seemed to be answering anyway. Soon enough he would confront her with his decision, whether she liked it or not.

fifteen

Sarah's Saturday at her folks' place in Litchfield brought her closer to those she seldom saw. She attended church Sunday morning with her entire family. She enjoyed seeing how her brother's children had grown since their last visit.

When the service ended, she and Amanda met outside with a warm hug. "It's so good to see you."

Sarah laughed. "We live too far apart. Why don't you move closer?"

Amanda's frown didn't hide the amusement in her eyes. "I should move? Hey, this works both ways, you know."

Sarah sighed. "I know and sometimes I'm tempted. Listen, I've got to go. My folks are waiting to go to Grandma's. Have you heard from Tessa?"

"Yes, she and her family will arrive late tonight. We won't see her until tomorrow, but we'll have a long talk then. We'll spend the entire day together—the three of us."

"I'm counting on it." Sarah stepped away. "I've got a family reunion this afternoon, or I'd sneak over today. I'll see you tomorrow."

Monday, July the Fourth, Sarah lifted her face to a gentle, cooling breeze that helped offset the hot summer sun already warming the Davises' backyard. After inhaling the tantalizing aroma of grilled hamburgers, she let herself into the kitchen and deposited her cake on the table.

"Sarah's here." Amanda, looking like a teenager with her reddish brown hair up in a ponytail, skillfully sidestepped two of her parents' neighbors to share a hug. "What took you so long?"

"This cake." Sarah pushed her cake against another dish. "Where's all this food coming from? There's no room for more."

"My boys aren't complaining." Tessa appeared beside them after waiting for a path to clear. "Do you always invite the entire town, though? I can't remember this many people."

"Maybe because it's been ages since you showed up." Sarah hugged Tessa.

Amanda said, "The three of us together. This is great. The way I wish we could be all the time. We started out here in Litchfield together, then scattered from Chicago to Amarillo to Los Angeles. Yet in our separation we have grown closer than we might have been if we'd stayed right here seeing each other every day. What we hold in our hands often becomes commonplace, while we value most that which we work for the hardest. I think that's the way our friendship is. I value you, Sarah, and you, Tessa. So much."

Sarah saw the pain in Amanda's eyes. Losing her husband and daughter four years ago had been hard on Amanda, but Sarah didn't want unhappiness intruding on their time together. She squeezed her friends' hands and smiled. "I agree, but if you get too serious, I'm going to cry."

Tessa gave an exaggerated sniff. "Yeah, me, too."

They laughed.

Amanda groaned. "Oh no. We should have run away. Sarah, your mom's with my mom, and they're coming this way."

"I see you girls found each other." Brenda Davis smiled at them. "Linda, remember when these three were in junior high and made the rounds from one house to another having sleepovers?"

Sarah's mother laughed. "I sure do, only I don't remember much sleeping going on. Tessa, did Deloris come with you?"

"No," Tessa shook her head. "Mom's still a newlywed, you know. She and Clark seldom go anywhere."

"Well, be sure and tell her we miss seeing her." Brenda smiled and patted Tessa's arm. "You don't know how good seeing you girls together is. I know it's a long way for you to come, Tessa. Thank you for making the effort. And you, too, Sarah."

The mothers moved on, and Sarah turned to her friends. "Okay, do we brave the wide-open spaces where men, women, and children can stop us every two minutes, or shall we hole away in Amanda's air-conditioned bedroom?"

"May I have your attention?" Amanda's dad stepped inside the kitchen door and held his hand up. Several groups of women visiting around the room grew quiet and turned to listen, including the circle of three friends. He grinned. "The meat line is forming as I speak. We're asking everyone to join us outside for prayer before we serve. After that, if you volunteered to serve in here, better get in place because the hungry masses will soon swarm. If not, you might want to find a place in line."

"Come on, ladies." Amanda headed toward the door. "My family may host this shindig, but I don't serve unless I have to."

Sarah fell in behind her and Tessa muttered, "We're with you. Let's get in line before we get volunteered."

Although Sarah longed for privacy to visit with her two best friends, someone continually stopped one or all of the women to catch up on their lives. Three hours later, after many of the guests left, they found solace in Amanda's upstairs bedroom as Sarah remembered doing so many times in the past.

Sarah stepped inside the room, which looked the same as it had when they were teenagers. Amanda closed the door and looked at Tessa. "You won't get in any trouble with your husband, will you?"

Tessa's eyes softened when she smiled. "No. Blake, or I

guess I should say Rob, took them for a drive to check out the town. They won't miss me until they're hungry, and maybe not then since Blake's better in a kitchen than I am." She cocked her head to the side as if thinking. "In fact, so is Rob."

Sarah laughed. "You've got to be kidding. After all they ate?"

Tessa perched on the edge of Amanda's full-sized bed. "Oh Sarah, you've seen my boys in action. Have you forgotten?"

"Yeah, I guess you're right." Sarah remembered the week they'd spent with her last summer in Chicago. She climbed on the bed and sat with her legs crossed. "So Amanda, what's going on with school?"

Amanda took a corner of the bed and faced the others. "Well, like I told you, I'm taking the summer off because I only need another nine hours. I should be done by January, and then I start sending out job inquiries."

"In early childhood, right?" Tessa asked. "What grades does that include?"

Amanda shrugged. "I'll be certified through third grade, but I think I'd like kindergarten. What do you think?"

"What else?" Sarah laughed. "You'll be one fantastic kindergarten teacher. I'm so proud of you."

"Definitely," Tessa agreed.

"So how's your life?" Amanda asked Tessa.

Tessa laughed. "I praise God every day for Blake and the boys. They are such a blessing in my life. I watch Blake with our sons and see the father they never had. Derek is his by blood, but Seth and Rob are sons in his heart and in theirs. His parents are the same way. They never make a difference in them, and the boys love them for it. I have a good life that I treasure."

"Sarah?" Amanda reached for Sarah's hand. "What's wrong? Is it Trey?"

Tears she couldn't stop rolled down Sarah's cheeks. They'd been having so much fun, and now, listening to the others with their lives settled and blessed sent her thoughts into a jumbled, hurtful spiral. At Amanda's question, she shook her head.

"No, Trey is wonderful. He's so much more than I could have dreamed." Her breath caught in a hiccup as she tried to keep from crying. "He told me he may become a preacher. Isn't that wonderful?"

"Of course it is." Tessa moved to hold Sarah's other hand. "What about Kevin? What has he done?"

Tessa sounded so defensive that Sarah almost laughed. She would have if a sob hadn't gotten in the way. She shook her head. "Nothing. He's been nicer than I thought he could be. I told you about Marilee's Home."

Both friends nodded.

"I've been reading the Bible Trey gave me. I feel so mixed up and empty inside." She bowed her head and pulled her hands from her friends to clutch them against her middle. "I thought Kevin would fill the void he left so long ago, but he won't."

"He can't, Sarah." Tessa touched her knee. "That hole you're talking about is God-shaped. Nothing else will fit."

Tears flowed at Tessa's soft words. Sarah covered her face with her hands. "Help me. Please, I need your prayers."

Amanda scooted closer and put her arm around Sarah's shoulders. She began to pray, while Tessa talked. Sarah had never been more ready to turn her life over to the Father. She'd served Him as a child; now she opened the door she had closed between them and rededicated her life to Christ with a commitment she intended to keep.

❧

Sunday morning before the Fourth, Kevin sat beside Trey in church and listened to the sermon taken from the third chapter of John. " 'Except a man be born again, he cannot see the kingdom of God.' " The minister's voice rang with conviction as he turned to the twenty-first chapter of Revelation and read the description of heaven. Then in chapter three: " 'I stand at the door, and knock: if any man hear my voice, and open the door, I will come in to him, and will sup with him, and he with me.' "

As the minister preached, the words burned Kevin's heart and described his life. Then the minister stepped down to stand in front of the congregation with his hand outstretched as if beckoning them forward. "He's standing at your heart's door knocking. Invite Jesus in."

An organ played in the background while the minister pleaded, "Softly, tenderly Jesus is calling. Come to the altar, and we'll pray with you."

The congregation stood and began to sing the old song. Trey leaned toward Kevin and whispered, "Everyone must receive the call to accept Jesus' forgiveness. Do you want to pray?"

Kevin wanted to run. Instead he nodded.

"I'll go with you."

Trey's offer and shift into the aisle was a lifeline pulling Kevin forward. He couldn't have stopped if he'd tried. He knelt at the altar beside Trey while tears filled his eyes and God's love filled his heart. For the first time in his life, he felt complete.

sixteen

At three o'clock Tuesday afternoon, Sarah stepped from her office with a smile on her face. "Tricia, I have an errand I need to run. I'll see you in the morning."

As Sarah left the hospital and drove across town, misgivings fluttered like butterflies in her stomach. Would Kevin listen to her if he was even there? What if Miss Parker was with him? She had to take the chance. She had to tell him about her commitment to Christ; then tonight she'd call Trey. He'd rejoice with her.

Sarah knocked on the door she'd been told was Kevin's.

"Come in."

"Kevin?" She pushed the door open.

He stood while a slow smile lit his face; his eyes welcomed her. "Sarah?"

"May I talk to you?" She still hesitated at the door. Her heart fluttered like a bird ready to take flight.

"Sure, come on in." He moved away from the desk and stepped forward. "Please, have a chair."

Sarah sat while he closed the door. He perched on the corner of the desk near her. "What brings you out here?"

"I have something to tell you. I went home over the weekend and found what Trey's been trying to tell us. I want to share with you, Kevin." Sarah smiled as her newfound joy bubbled from her heart. "At the Davises' cookout, Tessa and Amanda prayed with me. I committed my life to the Lord, Kevin. I don't know how to explain it, but it's wonderful to know my life's in His hands now."

Kevin threw back his head and laughed. Sarah frowned.

How could he laugh at her when she'd risked so much coming to help him see the truth? She stood to leave, but he caught her hand in his.

"Don't go. I'm laughing because you don't have to explain anything to me. I spent the weekend with Trey. I went to church with him, Sarah. But that's not all. I, too, accepted God's gift of salvation. I laughed because I'm so happy for you and for me."

"Oh, Kevin." Sarah's laughter joined his before a quick knock on the door intruded.

She dropped his hand and stepped back. Valerie Parker walked in with a file folder in her hands.

"Oh." Sarah had almost forgotten about Kevin's girlfriend, or was she his fiancée now? "I need to go."

"Don't leave on my account." Valerie glared at Sarah. Ice crystals glistened in her words. "I'm just delivering this folder to Mr. Nichols."

She walked out the door, head held high. What had happened to her? Sarah turned to question Kevin and met his mischievous grin.

"Valerie isn't too happy about some decisions I've made." He shrugged. "She's used to getting whatever she wants. For some reason she wanted me, and I said no."

He took Sarah's left hand and lifted it as his words soaked in, distracting her. "I don't see a ring here. What's going on?"

The warmth of his hand on hers crept to her heart. "Oh, that ring you found? I never wore it. Never even tried it on. In fact, if you'd given me a chance to tell you, you would've known I never intended to. I gave it back to Harold and then cried on his shoulder over you."

She watched his expression change from pain to disbelief to jealousy as she talked. His scowl became fierce as he growled, "If you need a shoulder to cry on, it'd better be mine from now on."

Sarah laughed, and his frown disappeared as he said, "I'm taking you out tonight. Wear something nice."

"Yes, Kevin." Sarah spun away from him and hurried out the door before he could stop her. She heard his laughter as she walked away.

&.

Sarah slipped into the most romantic dress she owned. She lifted the filmy skirt out to each side and twirled around in front of her full-length mirror. The royal blue made her eyes look like pools of Michigan Lake reflecting the summer sky. At least she hoped Kevin would think so. She laughed and twirled once more as the doorbell rang.

Her heart beat out a rhythm for her feet as she danced downstairs and pulled the door open.

Kevin handed her a dozen red roses with a smile that circled her heart and lit his eyes as he took in her appearance. "You're beautiful, Sarah."

She could've said the same for him. He wore a suit without a tie. He'd left the top two buttons of his shirt open, giving him a roguishly handsome look. She pressed her right palm over her heart to still its pounding. "Thank you. I'll put these in water."

They ate at Latarini's. Kevin had always been a gentleman, but tonight he made sure her every need was met immediately. Not that it would have mattered. Just being with him was enough. Since they'd shared their newfound commitment to serving the Lord, a bond between them had been forged that could not be broken. Her love for him had never been truer, and she sensed the same from him.

They left the restaurant and headed east. Were they going to the Lake? She didn't care. She just didn't want the fairy-tale evening to end.

When Kevin pulled to a stop at Grant Park, Sarah knew what he had in mind. Buckingham Fountain. He'd promised to bring her at night so they could watch the water spray in the multicolored lights.

Kevin opened her car door and reached for her hand, which she gladly gave. Side-by-side they followed the path to the fountain. Hand-in-hand they watched the beauty of the water and the fountain. The four seahorse statues representing the four states that touched the lake. The colorful lights, the music. All of it together couldn't have created a more romantic moment for her.

Kevin turned to face Sarah. She watched the water arch above and behind him in a spectacular display; then she only saw Kevin and the love in his eyes.

"I've accepted a job in real estate."

His words surprised her. "You're leaving Parkers?"

"Oh yeah." He grinned. "When I made it clear I didn't want the daughter, the job lost its appeal. I've got another week to go, and then I get to play in what I really enjoy. Only I'll have a salary as well as commission. I think it's a good choice."

"That's wonderful." That he didn't want Miss Parker. Maybe changing jobs, too.

"But that isn't all." His grin disappeared, and his eyes darkened as he searched her face. "I love you, Sarah. I always have. I walked away from you twice, but I never stopped loving you. Not even once. Can you forgive me?"

She swayed toward him. The night, bright lights from the fountain, Kevin so close. He could ask her to forgive anything tonight and she would. Only love filled her heart. "Yes, if you'll forgive me."

He released her hand and caught her by the shoulders.

"You were never at fault. Unless you can be blamed for letting me walk away." He smiled. "Will you marry me? If you say no, that will be the second huge mistake of our lives."

"Yes."

His eyes shone. "Yes, you will?"

Love stretched toward every corner of her heart. She lifted her lips as he pulled her close. "Yes, more than anything I want to be your wife."

Their lips touched in a sweet kiss. Mist from the fountain drifted over them as the wind shifted. Kevin pulled back and smiled at Sarah. "Can we take that as God's blessing?"

She smiled. "I think so."

They kissed again and Kevin murmured, "Let's get married real soon."

"Oh yes, before Trey goes to college. We've wasted entirely too much time already." Sarah lifted her lips for another kiss.

❧

Sarah stood at long last beside the only man she would ever love as they said their vows. The minister turned to her.

"Do you, Sarah Anne Maddox, take this man, Kevin Nichols, to be your lawfully wedded husband?"

"I do."

"Do you have a ring?"

Kevin turned as Trey, standing tall and handsome beside him, handed him the ring. His hands were steady and warm when he slipped the ring on Sarah's finger.

Then she placed a ring on his finger, and together they repeated their vows.

"I now pronounce you husband and wife."

Sarah's heart soared with love for Kevin. For the boy she'd never stopped loving, but mostly for the man he'd become.

"You may kiss the bride."

"I will cherish you always," Kevin whispered before he claimed her in the sweetest kiss she'd ever known.

"I love you, Kevin," Sarah murmured. Together they faced the crowded church in Litchfield, Illinois.

"May I present Mr. and Mrs. Kevin Nichols?"

Music swelled as the wedding party hurried down the aisle toward the fellowship room in back to receive congratulations from their friends and families. Kevin's parents stopped with wide smiles on their faces. Both hugged Kevin first and then Sarah.

Sincerity shone from Mrs. Nichols's eyes when she said, "Sarah, I'm glad you're part of our family now. We need to get together sometime and shop. I can't think of a better way to get acquainted."

Sarah laughed. "I couldn't agree with you more. Give me a call anytime."

Kevin gave her a quick hug. She smiled then watched her new in-laws shake Trey's hand.

Mrs. Nichols said, "I understand if you don't want to think of us as your grandparents. We've made plenty of mistakes in our lives, but. . ."

When she left her thought hanging, Trey smiled at her and said, "We all make mistakes, but I know the One who brings joy from ashes. Mistakes can always be forgiven."

When he opened his arms to hug his grandmother for the first time, Sarah exchanged a smile with her husband and whispered, "I hope mother pride isn't a sin, because I couldn't be prouder of our son."

"How about father pride?" His grin widened. "Or husband pride? You're pretty special, too, you know."

"Maybe it isn't pride at all. Maybe it's love."

He pulled her close. "Oh, it's definitely love."

&

As the reception drew to a close, Sarah changed from her wedding dress into comfortable slacks and a short-sleeved cotton blouse. Before they left the ladies' restroom, she hugged her best friends. "Thank you for everything. Especially for being with me today. In less than two months, you both made the long trip to be here. That means so much. I love you, Tessa. I love you, Amanda. You're the best friends anyone could have."

"You would do the same for us." Amanda brushed off her words.

"That's right," Tessa agreed. "You were at my wedding, weren't you?"

"Of course. Texas isn't so far away." Sarah turned toward Amanda with a teasing grin. "California isn't much farther, you know."

Amanda laughed and pushed the door open. "Remember that when you come for a visit. Just don't expect another wedding from me."

She let the door close behind her. Tessa's eyebrows rose. "Was that a prayer request?"

Sarah tapped her chin with one finger. "You know, I think it was. But as my son says, we must pray for God's will above all."

"Definitely."

Tessa and Sarah followed Amanda.

⁂

Sarah loved the possessive feel of Kevin's fingers interlaced with hers as they prepared to leave the church.

Trey stopped them near the door. "Hey, I want to say thank you for so many things." He shrugged. "I mean the car is beyond cool, but well, I wouldn't be here if it weren't for you. Thanks for giving me a chance at life. Thanks for letting Mom and Dad adopt me. Thanks for caring enough to meet me and become my friends. You know what I'm trying to say."

Sarah couldn't stop a tear from sliding down her cheek. She brushed it away and smiled as she took the tall boy in her arms. "Maybe you haven't realized, but you've given us life, too. Without your prayers and words of encouragement, we'd still be lost in our complacency. We wouldn't have each other, and we wouldn't have the Lord living in our lives. Thank you, Trey."

"That's right." Kevin stepped forward and, with one arm

around Sarah, clapped Trey's shoulder. "We may not be a family like we could've been, but because of God's forgiveness, we are family and always will be. Thanks, Trey. We owe you."

A sly smile crossed Trey's face as he looked from Kevin to Sarah. "There's one way you could pay me back. I never liked being an only child. I wouldn't mind having a little brother or sister to play with once in a while."

Kevin's laughter joined Sarah's. He hugged her close. "Now that's an idea. Guess we'll leave it in God's hands."

Trey grinned. "Fair enough."

author notes

Kevin Nichols is not a cook, and neither am I, but my oldest son is, and this is his easy version of a favorite. It would be hard to mess this up, yet it tastes great and never lasts long. It's also a great way to use up leftover vegetables and mashed potatoes.

Shepherd's Pie

1 can mushroom soup
½ cup milk
1½ pounds ground beef, venison, or turkey, browned and
    drained
1 can drained green beans, corn, peas, or carrots
8–10 potatoes, peeled, boiled, and mashed
⅓ cup grated Parmesan cheese, if desired
season as desired

Add mushroom soup and milk to cooked ground beef and mix thoroughly. Line casserole dish with meat mixture. Pour drained vegetables over meat. Cover with mashed potatoes, spreading to edge of dish. Sprinkle with Parmesan cheese if desired. Bake at 350 degrees until potatoes are lightly browned.

A Letter To Our Readers

Dear Reader:
In order that we might better contribute to your reading enjoyment, we would appreciate your taking a few minutes to respond to the following questions. We welcome your comments and read each form and letter we receive. When completed, please return to the following:

Fiction Editor
Heartsong Presents
PO Box 719
Uhrichsville, Ohio 44683

1. Did you enjoy reading *Redeeming Sarah's Present* by Mildred Colvin?
   ❏ Very much! I would like to see more books by this author!
   ❏ Moderately. I would have enjoyed it more if

   _____

   _____

   _____

2. Are you a member of **Heartsong Presents**? ❏ Yes ❏ No
   If no, where did you purchase this book? _____

   _____

3. How would you rate, on a scale from 1 (poor) to 5 (superior), the cover design? _____

4. On a scale from 1 (poor) to 10 (superior), please rate the following elements.

   ____ Heroine   ____ Plot
   ____ Hero   ____ Inspirational theme
   ____ Setting   ____ Secondary characters

5. These characters were special because? _____
   _____
   _____

6. How has this book inspired your life? _____
   _____
   _____

7. What settings would you like to see covered in future
   Heartsong Presents books? _____
   _____
   _____

8. What are some inspirational themes you would like to see
   treated in future books? _____
   _____
   _____

9. Would you be interested in reading other **Heartsong
   Presents** titles? ❑ Yes ❑ No

10. Please check your age range:
   ❑ Under 18   ❑ 18-24
   ❑ 25-34   ❑ 35-45
   ❑ 46-55   ❑ Over 55

Name _____
Occupation _____
Address _____
City, State, Zip_____
E-mail _____